ABOUT THIS BOOK

In this sequel to *The Winged & the Wicked*, Teeny Weeny is off to save her little mermaid friend in another Teeny Weeny Fairy Tale.

Teeny Weeny Tahini's life had always been quiet and simple, just the way she liked it. At least, until a year and a half ago, when her owl-shifter nephew Mat came to town with trouble on his heels. She and her extraordinary friends saved the day, but their happily ever after was short-lived. Now, the spring faerie has been haunted not only by nightmares, but also her past.

Compelled to travel thousands of miles to her ancestral home, Teeny Weeny leaves the safety and security of Havenwood Falls for the Isle of Gwynf'l, off the coast of England. Coralie, her long-time mermaid friend, is in danger, and the only way to save her is to take her back to Havenwood Falls. A series of obstacles combined with personal dilemmas from Teeny's past make it a foreboding journey, but one she must endure.

Traveling with a mermaid isn't easy, and the return trip could be racked with more problems because of the town's protective wards that only give her a lunar cycle away from her safe haven. Teeny Weeny and Coralie, not to mention a few uninvited travelers, race against time before they lose all memories of the place they now call home.

HAVENWOOD FALLS BOOKS

Betrayal Among the Frost by Amy Hale

Forever Loyal by E.J. Fechenda

Fate's Demand by Emily Cyr

The Wu & the Wand by T.V. Hahn

A Demon's Redemption by JD Nelson

Also try the YA line, Havenwood Falls High; the historical paranormal line, Legends of Havenwood Falls; the darker, sexier side of town, Havenwood Falls Sin & Silk; and the local supernatural college, Sun & Moon Academy.

Stay up to date at www.HavenwoodFalls.com

THE WARD & THE WANDERERS

A HAVENWOOD FALLS NOVELLA

T.V. HAHN

This book is dedicated to my husband "Bob," whose patience with my pixie life and endurance of reading everything I write (even the drafts) makes me adore him even more.

PROLOGUE

"FATHER, NO!"

"Siobhan, stay out of this. Your brother has disobeyed the code, and for that he must be punished."

My mother stood beside my father, crestfallen and bereaved.

Grenfold stood firm, silent, accepting of his fate. If he only knew.

My father chanted the code. "We, this family of fae, are of earth and air. When sea mixes with earth, it becomes mud. When sea mixes with air, tears fall from the heavens. You have brought both to this family. To be true, from this day hence, no longer are you fae, a prince. For your crime I extol, from this day forward, your life, a troll."

With that, King Ian—for he acted as king now, and not as a loving father —waved his royal wand above my brother's head, and the glowing orb at its tip touched my brother's brow. The first sounds Grenfold made since the commencement of this ghastly ceremony—which was unfairly replacing our usual festive Rites of Spring—were of such pain and agony that nothing human could compare to what my once beautiful brother was suffering. I knew this because over the years, as an empath, I had felt human pain, and this was something far beyond it.

The decibels and frequencies of my brother's cries were otherworldly as his body was transformed. The graceful, perfect frame of the handsome prince made a grotesque crunching of bones as his back disintegrated into a warped spine. My brother's cries and the horrific crackling of cartilage rocked the Isle of Gwynf'l to its core. His hands and feet became gnarled and twisted. His gorgeous golden locks fell in clumps from his head to be replaced by a wiry configuration of corkscrew strands, and even those had a resonance that I could taste as acrid and fuzzy on my tongue. His bright hazel eyes became like lumps of coal placed in a bed of gray clay, as his handsome features distorted. His nose became a long crooked probe with crusty warts, and his mouth turned and twisted, totally malformed, filled with protruding and decayed teeth.

After this horrible transformation was complete, my father, the great King Ian, ordered the troll to find a rock to crawl under.

And so he did.

My mother, the kind and generous Queen Rose, was so heartbroken, she turned ill and died within a few short months after Grenfold's departure.

Such is the price one pays for love. It didn't seem right that a gift of love should be so painful, so costly.

CHAPTER 1

The tinkling of the shopkeeper's bell rang sweetly in the dining room of Broastful Brew as I entered and slowly closed the shop door behind me, accidentally allowing a brisk March wind to add a bit of chill to the café. I trudged into the toasty coffee house and made my way to the back table, where my best friend, Barbie Stuart, the mayor of Havenwood Falls, sat sipping a simmering cup of coffee.

Havenwood Falls was no ordinary Colorado town. Oh sure, it looked like your typical frontier Victorian village one could find nestled in just about any canyon in the state, with the sun rays glistening off the golden aspens' fluttering leaves and the scent of pine wafting in the cool breeze. I could assure you, however, that was just a façade. Behind the brick and mortar, wood shingles, and gingerbread lattice work was a town full of supernaturals, from vampires and demons to werewolves and angels. In fact, I was one of them, a spring fae.

Not all of the townsfolk were supernaturals. The ratio varied from time to time, ranging between forty and sixty percent supes. I think it depended on how the stars aligned, but I could be wrong. There could be something much more mysterious behind the mix.

Regardless, the town was founded by the Old Families, one of which was mine. We were—and yes, some of us are still quite alive and kicking—supernaturals looking for a safe haven, where our supernatural abilities would not subject us to prejudice, as we discovered would happen just about anywhere else.

The founders created the town and the government known as the Court of the Sun and the Moon. All of the Old Families had one member sitting on the Court. I held my family's seat, although I was basically the wallflower of the group most of the time.

The Luna Coven created most of the magic that protected Havenwood Falls, including something the town referred to as the "memory ward." As soon as a visitor traveled outside of the twenty-five mile radius of the town's limits, their memory of our little haven vanished. The residents got a bit of a reprieve on this mystic cloak, in that we could exit town for one complete moon phase—twenty-eight days—before our memories of Havenwood Falls disappeared.

I found Havenwood Falls serene and comforting, and really never had any reason to go anywhere outside of its protective borders. Others—a Roca here and a Bishop there—seemed to have a necessity to come and go frequently.

I withdrew the chair from the table when the mayor looked up at me. She was visibly startled at my appearance.

"Siobhan! You look dreadful! Is it the spring equinox that's bothering you? I've never seen you look so . . . well, so bad." Barbara, a dear friend and a member of another Old Family, invited me to join her.

Barbie had listened to me recount my family tale every spring for what seemed like a hundred years, and may very well have been. We met regularly at Broastful Brew. Unlike the bustling Coffee Haven, where the younger folk liked to hang, Mabel's coffee shop was quite sedate and the perfect place for us two to congregate.

Barbie's stature was so starkly different from mine, me being only four foot five, the town's mysterious palm reader and potion mixer, lovingly (I think) known as Madame "Teeny Weeny" Tahini. By contrast, Barbie's six-foot frame was not enough to intimidate, her bouffant beehive hairdo—which she sometimes dyed in various pastel colors according to her whimsy so it looked like a wand of cotton candy—added at least six more inches to her height.

Tahini was not really my surname. It was McFeeny, but being a palm reader and all, I felt Tahini gave it a much more exotic allure for my trade, and it rhymed with McFeeny. For that matter, it rhymed with Teeny Weeny, too.

Normally I was very cheerful and lighthearted, or so I'd been told. Barbie always said I had a childlike nature of wonderment drifting about me. However, this day my faerie glamour wasn't sparkling, dark circles rimmed my eyes, and my generally shiny long brunette hair was in a fizzled mess around my shoulders. I'd noticed the ghastly reflection in the glass door before I entered.

"I haven't been sleeping well, Barbie. I've been bombarded with nightmares. I can't make anything of them. It's just so weird for me. The Rites of Spring dream—I'm used to that. For so long, I've relived that moment, and I have wished I had the power to break my father's curse."

Barbie nodded with understanding, but she raised one eyebrow, as if she thought differently about my wish.

She wrapped her large soft hands around my tiny wringing fists, trying her best to comfort me.

"You poor dear," she said soothingly. "Maybe these nightmares stem from that awful incident with that Pisik cat-shifting witch and your poor nephew Mat. You are not so accustomed to commotion."

I smiled weakly at my friend's attempt at assonance—word play had always been one of my favorite forms of dialogue. But not so much today, or for the last week or so, for that matter.

"Tell me about the nightmare. It might help to talk it out. Maybe between the two of us, we can fathom its meaning," she prodded.

"Well the first one—" I started.

"First one! There's more?"

"Nightmarezzz," I exaggerated wearily, emphasizing the plural, then continued. "The first one starts out in the dead of winter. The snows have already fallen heavily in the canyon. I have effervesced and flown up to Peacock Lake. The triplet falls are frozen solid, and the lake is like a shining mirror. I'm barely able to discern any of its radiant colors. I am enjoying the crisp, fresh smell of the whiteness. The air is so clean, the scent of the pines is outright singing to me at Small's Falls. I am listening to the soft chords of the sunlight passing through the icicles on the falls' ledge, spraying the colors like a prism, a harp strumming angelic psalms across the lake. It's peaceful and serene, and I am enjoying the scenery."

I paused, then continued, "Suddenly, black irregular spots begin to appear across the snowy landscape. They grow bigger, dripping upon the land, as if something black and evil is clawing at the snow-laden mountains. The blackness runs like spilt ink, and the spots begin to run into one another, growing larger. The smell is so acrid, sticky, like the smell of crude oil, but worse, like deeper than those bowels of the earth. It is a smell so strong that I wake up drenched in sweat, unable to shake the odor from my nostrils and way too afraid to try to go back to sleep."

Barbie sat unblinkingly as she pondered the dream's description and sipped her coffee. Mabel had brought my usual pot of hot water and favorite chamomile tea in a bag. I half-heartedly bounced the teabag up and down in the pot, but I was just not really inclined to actually pour the tea into my cup.

"Not sure I can make much of that. *Yet.*" Barbie went on, "Normally, it doesn't sound like much to make such a sweat over —sorry, no pun intended. However, you do have that ultra-synesthesia thing going on. You know, where you *feel* smells so strongly, and *hear* colors so vividly, and a bunch of other mixed up senses, that it's perfectly understandable. Maybe it's connected to the next dream. Tell me about that one?"

There were not too many folks in town who knew the mayor had a talent for interpreting dreams. Maybe it was just her curiosity in netherworldly ways, or maybe an inheritance she had yet to expose.

Barbie was supposedly human, but I had my doubts, having known her for so long. Even with our long friendship, I had just learned some of her secrets at her last Thankshannamas gathering, when she thought she had lost her dragon pendant, a family relic that evidently gave her strength and agelessness when she wore it. I had noticed long before that she never changed, except, of course, for the mound of cotton candy that topped her crown. From time to time, her hair color had been pale blue, pale pink, pale yellow, pale purple, pale whatever, a pastel rainbow of sorts. The pale yellow must've been her favorite, at least when in public, but every now and again, she would get a little adventurous. And each color smelled like . . . well, pale blue like blueberry, pale yellow like lemon chiffon, etc. At least to me, which was yummy.

I remembered when she had it almost a lavender color, but lavender was not the scent I'd picked up. I'd had a hard time identifying it.

"Welch's grape juice," she'd remarked.

That was it! It smelled like grapes. Did she soak that magnificent head of hair in a vat of Welch's grape juice, or was it just her inspiration? I didn't know. Maybe someday she'd tell me.

But like I said, Barbie had never changed—other than the color of her hair—for decades. On the other hand, she had never exhibited any supernatural powers either, in public or to me, other than that ancient talent of dream interpretation. Then again, she did seem to have some superhuman strength, or I could be imagining it. Since she's so much larger than I am, her own human abilities might just be that strong in comparison to me having to use my faerie dust to accomplish something similar, like picking up beings twice my size, as an example.

She'd held so many different positions in town and on the Court, but had always been a major presence. And she was never without the dragon pendant (which most folks thought represented the high school mascot) that hung precariously from a silver chain around her neck, with its tail always pointing to a voluptuous cavern of cleavage, as she was very well-endowed.

As to her requesting me to tell her about the *next* dream, I obliged.

"So the next time, I dreamed I was sipping a delightful cup of tea in front of the blazing fireplace in the parlor of Whisper Falls Inn. Madame Luiza is sitting with me in her ghostly form, and we are having one of our lovely chats about the town's ancient history, and the miscreants that once inhabited our wonderful village, and the few who still do. You remember what it was like? We are having such fun, as Luiza describes so many of the colorful characters and their doings and misdoings. She saw and knew so much. It is always fun talking with her."

Barbie nodded her lemon-chiffon head, recollecting those chats herself, but waved her large beautiful hands in a come-forward gesture, begging me to continue.

So I did.

"The fire in the hearth suddenly crackles loudly, and fiery sparks fly out of the fireplace. We stand up immediately, trying to bat at the tiny sparks that could alight and place the entire inn in peril. Of course, Luiza is a ghost, so her batting is totally useless. A swirl of black smoke emits from the embers and circles throughout the room, thickening the air, making it nearly impossible to breathe. I am grasping at my chest, trying to gasp at least one more ounce of oxygen into my lungs before the horrific smog-like smoke takes over. There is a similarity in the smoky stench and that oily odor from the previous dream. At this point, I wake up, once again dripping with sweat, the pungent smell still burning in my nose and an ominous, dull ringing tone tolling in my ears."

Barbie sympathetically shook her head and patted my hands. "It's interesting that these dreams start out so . . . well, so dreamy. Then they kind of catch you off guard and take a sudden turn. So that's something to keep in mind. It might be that your dreams are foretelling the fortune teller something. Maybe you need to keep your guard up. Seems like you need to be on the alert."

"Yeah, you might be right, because the next one is like that too," I confided.

"Next one? You mean there's even more?" The mayor grimaced, realizing suddenly why I looked so miserable.

"One more, actually."

Barbie's brow raised higher than I thought capable, so I continued.

"I am back on the Isle of Gwynf'l with my parents and my brother, before, well, you know, before Father changed him. It is a beautiful day, and we are having a faerie picnic on the shore by the Bay of Gwynf'l. Mother has baked our favorite faerie cakes of honeysuckle honey and daisy flower flour. The pixies are skipping along the mollusk shells scattered on the beach and breaking out into their familiar wrestling matches in the sand. The waves are bright aqua topped with marshmallowy sea-foam, and they are gently lapping the shore. There are mountainous fluffy clouds in the sky, and they send sound waves of comforting lullabies and happy Irish ditties toward the sandy dunes that buffet the beach.

"I spot a waterspout forming out in the sea, and I am mesmerized by the sight of the swirling funnel, so magnificent in its perfect Fibonacci spiral. The funnel, though, is moving quickly closer and growing darker and larger. It is suddenly totally black as it reaches the shore, and a giant wave crashes over all of us, smelling like . . . Well, like before—oily, inky, black. And I awoke as soaked as if the wave had actually hit me, and this time I began to vomit from the odiferous air that surrounded me."

"This is not good, Siobhan! You should have called me earlier. We will have to be vigilant, since I am sure these are *warning* signs."

"But there's something else, also," Barbie continued. "I don't know if it's the smell or the black thing, maybe both. I will have to think more about this. No matter what, if you have another dream, you are to call me pronto, regardless of what time it is, understood?"

I nodded in acquiescence to Barbie's order, but my hands were still wringing one another and my teacup still remained empty.

"Drink your tea, hon. It'll help calm you. I have to run. I have a meeting at City Hall with a new visitor. I mean it about calling me!"

I shakily tried to pour the steeped tea from the pot into my cup as Barbie bent over to kiss the top of my head. I struggled to wiggle a few fingers in toodle-oo style, but it probably looked like a very disheartened farewell.

I did finish my tea at the Brew, albeit slowly, since my cup rattled every time I tried to lift it from the saucer, and I was fearful I would spill tea all over the place. I thanked Mabel for letting me sit so long, brooding. I guess today, it could be called Brooding Brew.

CHAPTER 2

$\mathcal{I}$ found myself mindlessly wandering through town square, as drab as my mood now that the Into the Mystic Psychic Fair had come and gone, the colorful tents and banners only a memory now. I wound up on the southeast corner, next to the gazebo, and decided to stop into Callie's Consignments, since Callie usually had something unusual in her inventory that could cheer me up a bit. Unfortunately, this morning I had difficulty concentrating on any of the fascinating items that always seemed to present themselves on the shelves and nooks of Callie's shop.

I did spot a new painting of a mermaid sunning herself on a rock as she preened her long red hair with a pearl-studded comb. The painting brought back the bittersweet memories of Gwynf'l and my friend Coralie, the beautiful sea maiden who, unlike her fellow merfolk, preferred to chat with the faeries rather than swim amongst her school.

This memory saddened me, though, as did my annual spring equinox recollection. I recalled how heartbroken Coralie was when she lost her love, my young faerie prince brother Grenfold. If only poor Coralie knew that Grenfold was not completely lost, just not a faerie prince any longer. I wasn't sure which was worse.

"Sorry, Callie, I'm a little distracted today. I'll come back when I'm in better spirits."

Callie Montgomery, the stunning-beyond-words olive-skinned gypsy demon, gently patted me on the shoulder, her multi-bangled wrist clinking a melody that looked like stars shooting around the room.

"No worries," she said as I exited the store.

I turned in the opposite direction from my own shop, Madame Tahini's Potions, Lotions, Palm Reading, and Other Extra-Sensory Services, and proceeded to the corner of the block, where the Haven Saloon loomed over the corner of the square.

I stopped and gazed at the frontier-style batwing doors of the saloon, and the sound of shattering glass and wooden chairs cracking on the floor of the saloon pierced my memory, as I reminisced about the brawl that Sheriff Ric Kasun broke up one of the last times I was there. The sheriff had a nose for trouble brewing. Must have been the wolf in him, literally. This did make him the perfect sheriff for our little town.

Maybe a shot of Irish Mist in my tea would fix me up . . . Tea and Sympathy. Maybe later.

Turning up Eighth Street, back in the direction of Broastful Brew, I strolled to the alleyway that led to Nina's Dress Perfect tailor shop. I climbed the steps that led to the second story tailor, but was greeted by a sign on the door that read *Closed*. I pulled my wool vest closer to my chest as I turned and descended the stairwell, not too disappointed, as I really wasn't in the mood to visit anyone, but was just trying to keep myself distracted. Besides, I knew in the back of my mind that it was unlikely Nina would be up at this early hour anyway, since she was quite a night owl.

I reluctantly returned home, as it was getting too cold for me to just wander about aimlessly. The winter winds started to whip up through the town square—even though it was already early spring—after all, these were the Rockies.

Retrieving the onyx-colored key from my vest pocket, I unlocked the front door, pulling the heavy engraved wooden plank toward me as I stepped into my townhome shop. I removed the vest and hung it on the coatrack in the foyer, then headed to the kitchen, which I always had decked out like a mad scientist's laboratory, with Bunsen burner, beakers and flasks, and an ancient apothecary's scale sitting on the kitchen counter where most people had their coffee maker and canisters. After all, I was a potion mixer, and these were essential tools.

I looked out the window over the kitchen sink and saw Cyllene, the dryad of Maximus. Maximus was an eight-hundred-year-old bristlecone pine that had been struck by lightning a decade or so ago, and the dryad was his soul. Cyllene was perched on the spearmint plant that still thrived in the window box, even throughout the harsh winter. A bit of a gift I had.

I opened the window, and the luminescent moth-like creature flew in gracefully, humming an indistinguishable buzz and whirr. I set up a funnel and clamp at the kitchen table, the little megaphone contraption I invented, and the nymph took her place of honor before the small end of the funnel.

"You're a sight for sore eyes, Silly Annie," I told her.

"Siobhan! It's Cyllene!"

"Yeah, yeah. See-Lee-Nee. Whatever, Silly Annie."

"Well, you are definitely *not* a sight for sore eyes! You look like a Terrible Teeny Weeny to me. In fact, you look like you have sore eyes. Are you sick? I haven't seen you for over a week. I've been worried about you."

"I've just had a few nights' bad sleep is all. Not for you to worry about." But I was concerned. Even more now, given Barbie's warning, but not knowing what I was supposed to be keeping my guard up against.

I spent a few hours that evening in my salon reading my first edition of Hans Christian Andersen's *Eventyr fortalte for børn—Fairy Tales for Children*. It was one of my favorites, and I'd been contemplating donating it to the Havenwood Falls Library, since the fire at the library had destroyed so many of the wonderful books that had been housed there. Many of the lost books had been contributed over a century ago by the founders, and since I was among the founding families, it seemed right to renew the tradition. But before I started getting all charitable and everything, especially with this prized possession, I thought I'd want to read it a couple more times.

I knew people thought these were fairy tales, but there was a lot of history and truth in the stories, and I was always reminded of one thing or another. I'd treated this book more like an encyclopedia of my family culture than a storytelling compilation.

Getting ready for bed, I picked out the pink flannel nightgown Nina had made for me. The flannel was so soft and thick, it felt like velvet. Only Nina could have found such a material as this. I finally felt a glimmer of coziness come over me as I climbed onto my thick feather mattress and pulled up the quilted duvet overstuffed with warm down.

A big yawn escaped my mouth as I reached over to turn off the Tiffany stained-glass lamp by the bedside and prayed to the spirits that tonight, at least one night, I would have a dreamless slumber.

That wasn't to occur.

I found myself walking into an unfamiliar village. There were thick oaks, maples, and pines surrounding the town. I could even feel the syrupy scent of maple in the air. It had the quaintness of a charming New England town, but no beings, human or otherwise, could be found, not even a squirrel or moose. It was so quiet and serene. As I entered the village, a wooden sign painted green and held up by two white posts greeted me. The gold lettering read *Welcome to the Historic Village of Fishkill – Settled in 1714.*

Near the center of the town stood a large two-story building of Georgian architecture with a cupola-topped turret attached on the right side. The lower story was white clapboard, while the upper story had brown wooden shingles on its walls. Beveled lettering above the entrance read *Van Wyck Hall.* There was a tall ladder that stood on the lower stoop of the entryway, leaning against the railing above the doorway, as if it was going to be used for restoring the sign.

I walked up the sidewalk to the town hall and ducked under the ladder that stood in front of the double doors of the building. On the left-hand door hung a small mirror for no apparent reason. As I reached to open the door of the hall, the mirror suddenly swung erratically, then flew off the door and shattered on the stoop into a dozen sparkling shards. I turned around to pick up one of the shards, and a small black cat with lime green eyes crossed my path. That bitter, pungent odor pierced my senses.

I sat up abruptly to find myself back in my feather bed, but the thick flannel nightgown was now sopping wet. I could barely catch my breath as I fumbled to turn the light on. I groped around some more on the nightstand and felt my cell phone on the stand. The phone read 5:11 a.m., but Barbie said anytime, "pronto," and that was an order, so I dialed 9-1-1.

The phone did not ring at the fire station, nor did it ring at the sheriff's office. My 9-1-1 was a direct hotline to the mayor, and of course, she picked up immediately.

"Siobhan, did you have another dream?" she asked without

even saying hello. She could probably hear my labored breathing over the connection.

"Oh yes, and it's like the others, dreamy at first then . . ." I went on to recite the details of this newest nocturnal haunting.

"Hmm . . . I think I've got it. Meet me at the Brew at seven o'clock sharp," Barbie told me, and hung up without waiting for a response.

CHAPTER 3

*I*pattered around the kitchen and salon for the next couple of hours, as the stench from that wicked dream would not dissipate enough for me to go back to sleep.

As it neared seven, I went back up to my room to dress, still feeling the dampness from the nightmare sweats. I pulled a black woolen long-sleeved dress from the armoire and placed a few ribbons, a dainty embroidered handkerchief, my ebony key, and a small silk packet of faerie dust (just in case—my personal motto) in the large blossomy pocket on the left hip of the dress. I bundled up a woven neck scarf and shoved it into the right hip pocket.

Downstairs in the foyer, I grabbed my wool vest with the fur collar from the coat rack. The fur pelt that Nina had fashioned into the collar was given to her compliments of Ranger Rusty, a bit of a lone wolf, but a very kind soul, from one of his hunts.

Pushing the door open to face the cold dark morning in Havenwood Falls, I stepped out, turned around to shut the door behind me, and locked it with the ebony key, dropping it back into my left pocket. I was keeping my guard up.

We both arrived at exactly the same time as Mabel was unlocking Broastful Brew's door.

"You two are earlier than usual this morning. It will take me a bit of time to get everything heated up. Sorry I'm so late, but I couldn't decide if I should put my thermals on this morning or if I was jumping the gun. Don't want to get overheated, you know, but then it's not worth catching a cold either." Mabel greeted us in her typically long-winded manner.

The shopkeeper's bell rang loudly as all three of us entered, and a brisk breeze blew through the door, throwing the small bell into a tizzy.

Barbie and I, looking much like the female versions of Mutt and Jeff, walked to our usual table, which should have a sign that said *Property of Mayors and Palm Readers*.

I was kind of hoping the black dress might detract from the dark circles under my eyes, but I don't think it helped very much. Barbie, on the other hand, looked stunning, perfectly manicured and made up as a model of Amazonian beauty would be, regardless of the early hour. A trait I admired about the mayor.

"Siobhan, do you remember right before we sent that Wicked Witch Pisik to her Carpathian rock, she said something?" Barbie began, shortly after the two of us had taken our seats. She wasn't wasting any time with small talk this morning.

"Sorta. I don't know that I caught all the words. It was a poem. Something about altitude and fish, didn't make any sense to me. I just figured it was her evil ranting madness."

"It was a poem, so to speak. Just as the black swirl of obliviation was about to whisk her away, she said, 'Altai's death I shall avenge. The fish will die as my revenge.'"

"Okay, I give. What's Altai? What's with the fish?"

"Altai was her lover, a snow leopard shifter. That's your ink spots on the snowy landscape in your first dream, remember?"

"Oh! Oh, my!" The skin on the back of my neck began to crawl.

Barbie continued to interpret the dream. "I believe the black smoke swirling in your Whisper Falls Inn dream and the black funnel cloud swirling in your Gwynf'l dream is the Pisik being swept off to her fate."

Now my entire body was beginning to get goose bumps, which for me felt like an extremely excruciating itch.

"I see. That makes sense, especially the smell. Remember when she first arrived, and I caught that awful scent when she came into Broastful Brew? I thought it was from the boys behind her, but they turned out to be her half-blooded brothers."

"Speaking of those two half-bloods—after they were defrocked, or should I say de-furred, by the Peacock Lake water and looked like two hairless sphinx cats, they were put up for adoption. Biddie Half-Moon, or maybe it was Irene Beckett, told me one of the hellhounds adopted them."

"Well, that's fitting—hounds and cats, ha! Okay, what about the other part of the Pisik poetry? 'The fish will die'? What do fish have to do with anything?"

"Ah, dear Teeny, your last dream put it all together for me. Your dream took place in a town called Fishkill. That's how I remembered what that wretched feline said. You hit three bad omens, just like your first three dreams. So the bad luck omens are walking under the ladder, breaking the mirror, then of all things a *black* cat crossing your path. Remember Shayin's evil background that Mat had shared with the Court? That the mermaid at Gwynf'l had drowned her precious Altai? So sad for Pisik," Barbie said with feigned sympathy for the terrible temptress, then she sighed again, knowing the heartbroken fate of poor Coralie. Barbie went on. "Not 'fish' plural in her little verse. It's *the* fish, meaning the mermaid," Barbie emphasized.

I nearly fell out of my chair as soon as I put two and two

together—or three and three (omens and dreams), in this case. That wicked Shay was planning on killing my friend Coralie! The obliviation spell that the Court cast upon Shay would make her unable to remember Havenwood Falls, but it could not protect Coralie in Gwynf'l.

Oh my gods and goddesses. I felt so guilty! I pled with the Court that day to obliviate, not obliterate, the Pisik. I hated to destroy anything, and through the centuries I'd come to realize that even when you did the right thing, there were unintentional consequences. Now it looked like my "right thing" had its unintentional consequences, this time another of Pisik's diabolical plots.

Here I go again. I began to wring my hands nervously, this time worried about how to keep Coralie safe from any gross ritual that creepy she-cat could concoct. *Keep my guard up? I'm going to have to* become *a guard.*

Barbie seemed to read my mind, as old friends often did. She patted my hand in that familiar gesture that I usually found so comforting.

"Maybe I should bring Coralie here to Havenwood Falls. That would certainly protect her from Pisik. Do you think I could? I'm not sure how, but maybe I can figure it out. Do you think the Court would allow it?"

Barbie smiled reassuringly. "I am sure the Court would allow it. Sounds like the only bad thing Coralie ever did was a good thing—get rid of a bad cat named Altai."

I brightened up for the first time in over a week and leaped up from my chair before Mabel could even come over with my tea bag and a pot of piping hot water. I couldn't help myself. I started jumping up and down with glee, like my normal faerie self, which made the mayor grin even wider.

"I've got to get to my salon and figure out what I will need for this adventure. Barbie, I love you!"

I had to pull out my handkerchief from my pocket to dab my eyes as they filled with tears of joy. I gleefully pulled on my winter vest and practically skipped out of Broastful Brew in such a delightful dance that Mabel didn't even scold me for not closing the door behind me.

I will have to contact Seamus. He's the only one who can get a hold of Coralie through her pearl. There is so much to do, I thought to myself, as I unlocked my door and entered the townhome. I lit the candle on the foyer table, and almost immediately the pumpkin-spice scent wrapped around me like a cozy blanket. I pushed through the draped beads and entered my palm-reading salon.

Nestled atop the large round table that was located in the center of the room and covered with a maroon brocade cloth was a glass sphere with a mysteriously whirling mist inside. I sat down in my overstuffed chair directly opposite the shop's storefront window. Gazing into the multi-colored orb, I began to chant, slowly and deliberately, taking deep breaths. "Tahini McFeeny, Famous Seamus," I repeated, over and over again.

The whirling colors inside the crystal ball began to turn into various shades of green, and a face came into view amongst the swirling mists of the globe.

"Ah, Siobhan, how is my dearest niece and favorite fae queen?" The baritone voice of my uncle Seamus came booming from the glass ball. I flinched at his use of *fae queen,* but I hoped he didn't see it.

"Good morn, Uncle Seamus, much better now, especially to see and hear you again. I need your help with a little communication, I think."

"Go on, little one."

"I need to bring Coralie to Havenwood Falls. I'm pretty sure she's in danger, and I think it's the best way to protect her."

"I am guessing that is probably true, since you saved my boy Mathew, and as we know, they both have a common enemy. But what about Grenfold? Will he be all right with that?"

I ignored his mention of my brother, as my only immediate thought was to protect Coralie from Pisik.

"Do you think you can contact her with your orb and her matched pearl? Let her know I will be coming for her within the fortnight?" I pleaded.

"For you, Siobhan, anything. I have not contacted her in very many moons, but she is never without her pearl, so I'm sure I can let her know. She will be so happy to see you. Just be careful. There may be more to protect against than just a demonic witch. Let me know if you need any other assistance. Make sure you take your sphere with you in case you need to get a hold of me."

"Thank you, Uncle! I will put the ball on the top of my to-do list. Kisses to Aunt Abigail. Speak soon!" I bade him farewell, blowing kisses at the rounded glass, as the face in the globe grew fainter and the green hues began to return to the myriad of rainbow colors it originally contained.

I swiveled my chair around to face the back wall and pulled on the tapestry that hung on it. The tapestry was like a pull cord for the drop-down door, revealing a recess in the wall that housed my computer. I tapped on a few keys, and the computer sprang to life.

I logged on to the Havenwood Falls residents' website and clicked the button that said *TW Only*. The browser re-directed me to the password reset page, to which only I and the other members of the Court of the Sun and the Moon had access.

I thought I'd better reset the password now, since I wasn't sure when my next opportunity would be. *Let's see. I'll be gone a couple of fortnights, so end of April or beginning of May. A May Day theme would be appropriate. I got it!*

I quickly typed out "mA¥pØ£€fA3R13f€5T"

That reminds me. I need to make some faerie cakes to leave for the pixies, just in case I'm not back before Spring Fest.

I created a new file on the computer called TO DO, and typed in:

1. Google Earth
2. Calendar
3. Faerie Cakes
4. Tell All Ball
5. Faerie Dust

Then I clicked save, logged off the computer, and closed the tapestried access door.

CHAPTER 4

I awoke after the first good night's sleep I'd had in weeks. I felt so refreshed in the morning and was anxious to put together the plan to rescue the endangered and forlorn Coralie.

I wasn't terribly creative, but I thought what I'd plotted out wasn't half bad.

I checked out Google Earth and estimated how far I would have to fly to get to Gwynf'l. Over 4,600 miles! Even though I could fly nearly 800 miles an hour, once I effervesced, I would need to make so many stops to replenish myself, as speeds that high eat up a lot of my energy. Shimmering was out of the question for that leg anyway, as the time warp is way too unpredictable—the Stipple in the Ripple. It was most likely best for me to take a plane to Belfast. Maybe the Court could supply me with a passport. I was hoping so.

I still had some family in Belfast, so I could ship whatever I needed to them first, like the Tell All Ball, and of course my stash of faerie dust. I needed to travel light and not mess around with airport security and all, so the shipping was better. I'd see if Addie could put a spell on the package, just in case it was scanned, so it appeared as if it only contained papers and books.

I could catch a fishing boat in Belfast to take me to the Isle of Gwynf'l.

This was going pretty well. Until I got to the point of how the heck I was supposed to get Coralie back here. I certainly couldn't expect her to swim all this way, especially in unfamiliar waters, and with so many waterways, rivers, and falls to maneuver.

I thought I might need the mayor's help on some of this, so I texted her a message to see if she could meet me at Broastful Brew.

So once again, we were at our table in the cozy coffee shop. This time I felt much perkier, and I was swinging my feet under my chair, because my legs were too short to meet the floor.

"Barbie, it's a long trip there and back again. I can fly like a faerie, but I doubt I could do the whole trip, especially over the Atlantic Ocean. There would be no place for me to rest. Let alone the fact that I'm not sure I can do it and be back again within a moon's full cycle. I may never be able to find Havenwood Falls again. But if I could get a passport, I could fly to Belfast. That would certainly speed things up a bit. Is that possible?"

"Not a problem. Come in to the Court and ask if they can give you some magic that will delay the effects of the wards. And yes, you can get a passport. After all, we are a government agency, don't you know?" Barbie said with a sly smile.

"Okay. I've already reset the internet password." I handed my dear friend a little slip of paper with the new secret phrase. "I'm pretty sure I've worked out getting there, but I'm not sure about getting Coralie back."

"Teeny, I have always believed that you underestimate your faerie magic. You will be able to do something to get Coralie back, I'm sure of that. Just don't forget to get the ward magic in place before you leave. The passport is easy. You can come over to City Hall anytime."

I wasn't so sure if she was right about my faerie magic. After Grenfold was turned and Mum died, I didn't want to have anything to do with fae magic or curses. Then when my father died, I only sprinkled a little dust now and then, since the pixies counted on me for that.

"You're probably right, Barbie. I'll just think positive."

I was even beginning to feel more positive. Barbie had already made arrangements for my upcoming departure. Now I had to get things packed up and ready to go.

When I returned home from Broastful Brew, I found four yammering pixies at my door. Enya was yanking on Ushka's hair, while Tierri was rabbit punching Aieri's arm. I opened the door as quickly as I could and shuffled them in before they could cause a scene on Main Street by breaking out into one of their notorious wrestling matches. Then Sheriff Kasun would be on their case and mine.

"Stop that, all of you! Where is your glamour anyway?"

Aieri shuffled her foot shyly in circles with her head down. "Oops, sorry, we forgot."

For the pixie sisters, their glamour was the closest thing they could come to manners.

"I have a lot to do today. I have to pack for a trip."

"A trip? Great! Where are we going?" Tierri asked, now jumping up and down, all excited.

"Is it a vacation?" Aieri, excited as well, rubbed the arm that Tierri had just moments ago used as a punching bag.

"Let's go to the Bahamas!" cried Enya, quickly joining the enthusiasm.

"Yeah! We could take the yeti too. HimaLaLa's in the Bahamas!" piped in Ushka. And of course, that little rhyme sent the pixies into a roar of laughter, rolling on the floor in my foyer. HimaLaLa was what they called the yeti that secretly lived in a cave with Gruff.

"It is *not* a vacation! And it is *not* we!" I stomped my foot to get their attention.

Suddenly, four small disappointed faces looked up at me. My heart dropped, but there was just no way I could risk their little lives on this strange journey I was about to embark on, especially when I was unsure how it was going to turn out.

I explained to the pixies that I had to go back to Gwynf'l, their homeland too, as it were, but it was too dangerous a trip for them to take, and I was going to be on a very tight schedule. I told them there was nothing there for them anyway, just sad memories.

"I should be back before the May Day fest, but I'll make some faerie cakes, and keep them in the freezer, just in case. Cyllene can let you in. She can get through the keyhole to unlock the door. And Mat has a key, so he can, too. Now why don't you help me pack?"

They all gleefully nodded their heads and scampered off into the kitchen.

I got a large box, some tape and string, and sent the pixies to gather bundles of loose paper to pad the box. Gathering things was a specialty of theirs: ribbons, strings, paper, and sometimes, carelessly, other people's jewelry.

I had printed off a calendar and marked what I thought would be a fairly accurate timeline. Even though the Court could help delay the ward's effects that would otherwise wipe my memory of Havenwood Falls, I didn't want to take any chances. Besides, I felt uncomfortable leaving the pixies for more than a month. I had a few ideas of what kind of trouble they could get into without supervision.

I placed the calendar in the box and went to get my crystal ball. I wrapped the brocade cloth that the ball sat upon carefully around the glass orb. There was plenty of cloth, but I said a small prayer to the spirits anyway that it would be protected.

When I returned to the box in the kitchen, the little sprites had already filled it halfway with balls of crumpled paper. I placed the covered sphere gently into the bed of padding.

Next, I went up to the attic to retrieve my stash of faerie dust. In the northwest corner of the attic sat the expertly handcrafted box made of various woods, smoothly polished and gleaming in the ray of light that cracked through the attic window. It was about fourteen inches long, five inches wide, and three inches deep. I passed my hand over the keyless latch of silver and abalone. The latch snapped open, and I inventoried my silk pouches of faerie dust, moving the small sachets about, and noticing the empty crevice in the bottom of the felt-lined box. The crevice seemed to have held something there long ago, but it was empty when my father gave me the box, telling me it was for my fae magic stuff. So I was never sure if that indentation was just a time-worn element or it was meant for something. Anyway, I was satisfied the dust was sufficient for my journey, so I closed up the box, passed my hand over the latch again, and it abruptly snapped shut.

I climbed down from the attic, released the access door, then went into my bedroom to get a silk scarf to wrap around the box and a few articles of clothing I would need for the trip.

By the time I returned, the packing box was now completely filled with paper balls, and there was no room for the items I had come down with.

"I need to put these in there too," I told them, holding up my armload of essentials in emphasis. "You will need to take some of this packing paper out."

With that, eight small hands began picking out the crumpled balls, and the next thing I knew they were lobbing them at one another, first as a game of catch, then they were throwing them at one another, then, yes, you guessed it, they were on the floor wrestling.

It's a pixie life. I sighed and shook my head. Once all the items were in the box and it was ready to close up, I realized I should cover it in craft paper, and went back up to the attic to get the large roll of brown wrapping paper. I could hear the pixies giggling and whispering, and could only hope they didn't make more of a mess before I came back down.

While up in the attic, I heard Enya holler up that they were leaving, and Ushka wishing me a safe trip, then Tierri's "me too" and Aieri's "me three." Of course, Enya added "me four." Another squeal of laughter, and I could hear the door slamming closed behind them.

Now where did I put that roll of craft paper?

I checked all the usual storage bins, and generally I was very organized, but it had been a very long time since I'd used it. At last, I found the cylinder under the bed that my "nephew" Mat had made his for a time.

I carried that back down the attic ladder, then down the stairs to the first floor. The kitchen was still strewn with paper, most of it in shreds now, but the pixies were gone, and a little peace and quiet was restored.

I sealed up the box, wrapped it in the craft paper, then tied it all securely with the string. With a black marker, I wrote my name on the package, then "c/o Rebecca Smyth" and her address. I would call her first to let her know to expect it.

The Smyth family was my second mother's family. I kept in touch with the family line through the ages, but because they were human, each time I had to tell the next family I was a descendant of Ian McFeeny and their great-great-great aunt, who was also a Rebecca. Mother Rebecca unfortunately died in childbirth, with a stillborn no less. It was great sadness for the Smyths, but each family had always been gracious to me, nevertheless.

After my father's marriage to Rebecca Smyth ended with her death, he found his next wife in Toronto, my third mother. After my mother's death and our exodus from Gwynf'l, the great King Ian was not so much the faerie king anymore. Once he met Rebecca, he found he had a penchant for the touch of human flesh, and just continued to marry one human woman after another, including my fifth mother, Tess, whom he had met in the States, and finally settled in Havenwood Falls. After Tess died, I guess my father just gave up, or maybe he really did love her, but he died only a few years later.

Cripes! I have to tell Gruff that I'm bringing Coralie to Havenwood Falls. Ugh, this is not going to be pleasant.

Father was going to leave Grenfold, now known as Gruff, under his rock when we were leaving Gwynf'l. This was the one and only time I stood up to my father. I refused to leave without him. Gruff would always be my family, even if Father disowned him. Even if he was a troll.

I picked up the package and carried it out the door, headed toward Addie's house. I was greeted by one of her familiars, a small dragon named Leia, who sniffed me up and down, then hopped off to get her mistress.

Oh my gosh, she's so adorable. I hope they're right, and she doesn't grow very big.

I explained to Addie that I needed to ship this package overseas, but it needed a spell so that its contents could not be detected. She asked me why didn't I just do it myself, since I could glamour anything with my faerie magic.

"I have to be in its presence to work the glamour. This package will be out of my powers' reach."

Addie was a whiz at all kinds of spells, being a Beaumont *and* an Augustine. Saundra, her grandmother, sat on the High Council of the Luna Coven, and had been grooming her for that position. Addie accepted the challenge, so I left the package with her and set off to see Gruff.

Once behind Addie's house, I looked around to make sure there were no humans that could see me, then I shimmered. The air around me began to waffle, and I started to become translucent, waving into that shimmering air, until I was more and more translucent, then completely gone.

My entrance at the front of Gruff's cave was the same as my exit from Addie's yard, but in reverse. As soon as I was opaque and the air stopped shimmering, I called out for him.

My dear malformed brother hobbled out of the cave. That little glimpse of light that flashed in his eyes when he saw me appeared briefly, before the black sullen lumps of coal took their place.

"Gruff, I have something to tell you. Please don't be mad at me." I could barely face him, but I mustered up the courage. "I'm going to Gwynf'l to bring Coralie back here."

That agonizing moan of centuries ago I had to endure again at this moment as Gruff's response echoed throughout his cave. The painful roar bounced off every rock and crevice in the hole.

He grabbed his head as if it were about to explode and could only say "NO NO NO," with his poor malformed mouth chock full of disfigured teeth.

"Gruff, I have to! Coralie's life is in danger. I have to . . . *We* have to protect her!"

Gruff's black eyes became glossy. Although the poor troll could not cry, it was evident he was weeping inside. "NO SEE ME!"

"No, I won't let her see you. I won't even tell her you're here, if you don't want me to. She doesn't even know you're still alive. I'm going to place her in Peacock Lake, so you may want to stay away from there. But we have to do this, okay?"

I felt my brother's heartache, his shame, his loss. I so wished there was some way I could help him. Some potion I could make to relieve his anguish.

Gruff just nodded reluctantly, sadly, and hobbled back into the cave.

I couldn't shimmer out of there fast enough. I felt so guilty, a lump caught in my throat, and my stomach knotted into a giant hard ball.

The shimmering knocked out a couple of hours in my day. That's a little problem with shimmering—there was stipple in that ripple—and I never knew if it was going to be a few minutes lost, or hours, or possibly even days. On occasion, it worked the opposite, and I would be given time to spare, or just have to wait until the rest of the world caught up with me. But not often, and I never knew which way it would go.

I had to get to the Court of the Sun and the Moon and get my passport before City Hall closed, and of course to request a delay in the memory ward, if possible.

I walked down Stuart to Eighth Street, then north to get to the entry behind City Hall. I pulled the heavy metal door emblazoned with the Court's insignia open, and pushed myself through the opening I had managed.

Lucky for me, Addie, or Adelaide Beaumont to the snooty old people, was at the door to the courtroom. She looked over her black-rimmed glasses, smiled, and waved at me to come over.

I still can't get the vision of her dressed up for Halloween as a sexy Stormtrooper out of my head.

"Okay, your package is spellbound!" she said, delighted with her own word play.

Even I laughed. "That's pretty good, Addie! I'm really running short of time. Could you possibly take this over to the OutPost for me?"

While the OutPost projected the image of a normal postal and overnight delivery store for the humans, Cerberus Delivery Inc. did the actual shipping in and out of town. CDI was kind of like Havenwood Falls' very own import/export company, owned by the leaders of an outlaw motorcycle gang, but we tended to ignore that little tidbit.

"Sure thing, Madame Tahini. Anything else you need?"

"I need to get a passport. Mayor Stuart said I could pick it up here."

Addie pointed to a door behind the Court's podium, and I followed her fingered direction. The courtroom was a "charming" place. Doors appeared and disappeared depending on their necessity.

Barbie was standing in the hallway, whispering with a ravishing caramel-skinned woman, whom I recognized as Qadira, the djinn that Roman Bishop had enslaved, though of course, I was not supposed to know that.

Barbie raised her right index finger to her lip when she spied my entrance. That was my signal that I never speak of this.

Yes, the scene looked a bit like a conspiracy. Barbie bade the amazingly sexy Qadira farewell, and I swear I heard both of them snicker, you know like that girlie confidante kind of snicker. Quadira poofed—vanished—and Barbie escorted me into a small room stationed just to the left of the door I had walked through just a few moments before.

As I entered, Roman stood up and held his arms out in a welcoming gesture, which was pretty scary, if you asked me. Like Barbie, he was perfectly manicured, and exquisitely suited to the max in what must have been a hand-tailored coat, probably Italian, but then his enterprise reached all over the world, so who knew.

Roman welcoming (and I used that term loosely) anyone other than a Bishop was more than just weird. He was usually surly and had no compunction to use his powerful mage abilities, even over other Court members. I was not about to offend him, so I walked into the small room to his opened-arm greeting, and gave him a perfunctory hug, as he wrapped his arms around my tiny frame in response. He was creeping me out.

Maybe he's on drugs?

"Barbara has been filling me in on some needs you have to make a trip across the pond. All we need now is a picture for your passport. We are quite up to date on the Homeland Security requirements, and since you've never had one issued to you, we of course have to alter a bit of your information, say like your date of birth! Haha!"

Roman making a joke was beyond a little eerie. But okay, though I did catch a little twitch under his left eye. *Is he lying or is he just uncomfortable?*

Barbie cleared her throat in an attention-getting way. It worked.

"Oh yeah, and I believe we have a little spell we need to expel so the ward doesn't get in the way of your wandering," he added, with another little strange chuckle.

He's definitely on drugs!

Roman had his own family, and they had their own issues. But this was soooo out of character for him to be pandering to me with his play on words that my skin was beginning to break out in those tiny foretelling bumps all over again.

Barbie rolled her eyes, gave me a quick knowing wink, then nodded and smiled. I wondered if she had made a pact with the devil here. However, the nod and smile was my cue that I was good to go.

Roman then instructed me to go to the room across the hall, where I could to take a "glamour shot" for my passport. Ugh, another pun from Roman?

It must've been Qadira. She had to have put a spell on him.

34

Brand new passport in hand, I was practically skipping home. As I crossed Town Square Park, I tossed a penny into the gold-flecked fountain and made a wish, just in case.

I was now ready to make my airline reservation. As soon as I got home, I went straight to my computer, pulled the tapestry access door down, and fired up the hard drive. I found a flight and booked a one-way ticket, since I wasn't exactly sure yet how I intended to get back home with Coralie. I then emailed my itinerary to Barbie.

In the parlor next to the kitchen, I lit a cozy fire in the hearth, sat down in the plush chair across from the fireplace, and pulled my cell phone out of my pocket. I dialed the overseas number for Rebecca Smyth. I hoped I wasn't calling too late, as it would be about nine p.m. there.

A lilting voice with a heavy Irish brogue answered the other end. "Smyth residence. Rebecca here."

"Hello, Rebecca! This is Siobhan McFeeny calling. How are you?"

"Siobhan, how lovely to hear from you. I'm doing quite well, thank you for asking. And you?"

"A bit busy lately. I have to make a trip to Belfast, and I'm on a tight schedule. I've sent a package to your home, if that's okay. Could you hold it for me until I arrive? I should be arriving Wednesday."

"Well, of course, my dear. It will be delightful to see you. Will you be staying here?"

"Oh no, just passing through, unfortunately. But I can certainly stay long enough to share a spot of tea."

We continued with a few pleasantries and catching up with her family tree. I bid farewell and placed my phone back in my pocket.

Closing my eyes for a moment, I basked in the warmth of the fire on my face, feeling pretty satisfied with my arrangements.

Yikes! I almost forgot. I still have to make faerie cakes for the pixie sisters.

Barbie called me first thing the next morning and offered to drive me to Denver International, knowing how likely I was to get motion sickness on the bus. I gladly accepted the offer, relieved but aware the canyon trip was still going to be a white-knuckled ride for me.

CHAPTER 5

The flight to the UK was uneventful and far more relaxing than the ride in Barbie's Maserati through the mountains. I had no idea how Barbie got the Maserati (and was sure I didn't want to know), or even how she managed to get her long legs and tall hair into the vehicle, but she did, and it seemed to suit her.

I was actually able to sleep some on the plane, with it being a red-eye flight. It worked out perfect for me landing at Heathrow. I only had a short layover, enough time to grab a breakfast tea and scone, before I picked up the second leg to Belfast.

Addie had downloaded the Uber and Lyft apps on my phone and showed me how to use them, so I wouldn't have to bother with exchange rates while moving around in a foreign country. The apps were so easy to use, and I had no idea there was such a thing, even though Addie said we had our own Luber in Havenwood Falls. How cool was that?

The apps came in handy when I arrived in Belfast. Only moments after going through customs, I was picked up by Evan, a blue-eyed redhead. I gave him Rebecca Smyth's address and was whisked off from the airport to a little section on the edge of the city. The driver said he couldn't take me all the way to the door, the road being one-way in the wrong direction, but it was only a few steps away from this intersection. I only had my carpet bag with me, and that was pretty lightweight, since most of what I needed was hopefully sitting in a carton at Rebecca's flat. I let him know I could easily walk it, and thanked him for the ride.

I rang the bell at Rebecca's door, and a diminutive young woman answered. She was just a few inches taller than me, unlike most of the Irish I had seen on the ride to her place. But it was no surprise, as my father had the small stature of the fae, and his tastes ran the same way when choosing his human brides, so that he appeared taller and stronger than those wonderful women.

Rebecca had the unblemished pale skin of her great, great ancestor, with just a small sprinkle of freckles across the bridge of her nose. She wrapped her arms around me, giving me a generous hug, then led me into her hallway.

I spied my package on the floor next to her entryway table, and was relieved that it had arrived safely.

Rebecca and I sat in her parlor for about an hour, sipping tea and reminiscing about our families. She pulled out an old family album, and all the women seemed to resemble the Rebecca I recalled as my second mother. It was so sad she died in childbirth along with her baby. Fortunately, she had a large family to carry on her memory.

After tea, Rebecca asked if I wanted to open the package. I told her it only contained papers and books, and nothing I really needed right away. It was light enough for me to carry, so I just needed to get to the fishing marina. I told her I had been researching my genealogy and discovered my father still had kin on the Isle of Gwynf'l, and I was headed there next.

Rebecca offered to take me to the marina, and I welcomed the invite, as I already had to deal with enough strangers in a strange land as it was. She dropped me off at the fisherman's pier, and I toddled my way down the deck with my carpet bag slung over my shoulder and my package in my arms. I asked a few of the fishermen if they knew where the Isle of Gwynf'l was. The first two just looked at me dumbfounded and shook their heads.

The third one, however, said, "Aye, go see Patrick at slip thirteen. E's gotta partner 'oo fishes outta da Bay o' Gwynf'l. Goes there of'en."

I thanked him profusely and scurried down to the slip numbered thirteen. Fortunately, Patrick was just loading up gear into his skiff.

I asked him if he could take me to the isle, and he informed me that it just so happened he was headed there today, and I could join him, no charge.

For his kindness, I slipped a little faerie dust onto his fishing rods while he wasn't looking, to give him some extra luck with his catch today.

The salt breeze was refreshing as we sailed through the Belfast harbor, down the strait and across the Irish Sea to get to the Isle of Gwynf'l.

Patrick had barely placed a hook into the waters when a great fish grabbed his bait and took off with what the poor fish thought would be a delightful breakfast. He even caught a huge king mackerel that was nearly half the size of me. Someone was eating well tonight.

The weather was cooperative, and the sails set just so to glide us toward our destination. It was truly great luck, since Patrick spent most of the expedition reeling one fish in right after another.

"Are you a leprechaun?" he asked me. "You even look like one, and you are certainly my lucky charm today."

I just smiled and wished him continued good luck.

Patrick sailed his small fishing boat up to the rickety pier in the small fisherman's village located on the Bay of Gwynf'l. His partner was waving at him, and Patrick was waving an overloaded skein of fish back at him, showing off his fantastic luck.

I again thanked the young fisherman, then daintily stepped out of the boat and onto the pier, my tapestried satchel over my shoulder and craft-paper-covered carton in hand, as his friend took my elbow to help me out.

I quickly made my way through the little village and wandered toward the hills in the north, where the shamrock glen bordered upon my ancient family home.

Alone in the glen, I sat on a large rock and began to untwine the wrapped package that held my precious items. Slowly, I pulled the tape off the packaging and folded back the craft paper to lift the lid off the box.

I was knocked off the rock by Enya and Tierri, who jumped out of the box screaming, "Surprise!"

Next, I found Aeiri and Ushka doing a jig around me, and all of them chanting, "I'm the Belle of Gwynf'l in the Dell of Gwynf'l!"

Wow! Did that bring back ancient memories. I taught them that little rhyme over half a millennium ago as they used to dance through the thick shamrock fields that flocked this glen.

"What have you done, you sneaky little stowaways? I have so much to do and so little time. How am I going to get back home in time, now that I have you munchkins to deal with?"

"We can help!" cried out Ushka.

"You need us!" stated Tierri, as she stomped her little pixie foot firmly on the ground.

The other two just mimicked the first two, then they all went back into their little jig and chant, as they picked through the field of green clover, sticking clumps of the three-leafed plants into their hair.

How I could use a four-leafed clover just about now, or maybe even a leprechaun to rein in these imps.

"I'm going to look around. Don't dare leave the glen!" I commanded the unwelcome travelers. They all giggled at me, then started a rumpus in the patch of shamrock. Okay, that would keep them busy for a while. And, generally, they were pretty good at following my orders; well, at least for a few minutes.

I was planning on heading up to my family's cottage, if it was still standing, which to our clan was the Crown Seat. Then I realized the rock the unexpected and exuberant pixie sisters knocked me off of was the same one my dear brother Grenfold, then turned into my poor Gruff, had crawled under as my father had ordered.

I thought maybe there might have been something under the rock that could ease some of poor pitiful Gruff's pain. Even after all these eons, I carried such tormented grief that there was nothing I could have done to stop my father from his cruel sentence. If I could have, then maybe Grenfold would still be my handsome, talented faerie brother and maybe the king of our fae, or my mother Rose and even my father might still have been alive. My heart ached so badly, I could hardly breathe.

The rock turned out to be, well, just a rock. There was a small gulley furrowed under it, which I assumed was formed by my brother's clawing and crawling. Just the thought of his damnation made my own fingernails hurt. I looked down at my hands, and there was blood and dirt crusted around my nails.

The empath in me returns.

The sun began to set in the west of the isle, but just as the glazing ball of gas was approaching the tips of the western mounts, a ray of light shone on something that gleamed in that gulley.

I forced my aching fingers down to the tip of that shining piece and felt a smooth round stone. It felt like there was some rod or branch attached to it. Regardless of the pain, I dug deeper with my bare hands into that gulch, and was able to grab the stick attached to the spherical rock that sat atop it.

I had to push my shoulder against the boulder, and I prayed to my faerie spirits to help me move it just enough.

I heard a thunderclap in the distance as the stone budged a centimeter or so, but lo, it was enough to get a grip on the handle of that stick and pull it out from where it had been buried for hundreds of years.

Thank you, spirits!

My shoulder ached, inflamed with the effort of pushing against that blasted boulder, but I held in my hand something I had not seen since that fateful day my father placed his curse on my brother.

The tip of my father's faerie wand! His king's scepter shone brightly in the fading sunlight, as if never encumbered by centuries of earth and rain. The staff was of finely polished ebony, a gift from his brethren of Belize, and that too remained unmarred.

Such is the way of fae wonders.

Some of my history started to make sense. After my mother Rose died, my father, other than gathering his clan and moving westward to the newfound land, never used his wand again. A bit of faerie dust here and there, when necessary, but I never saw his wand again.

I held the charmed scepter in my hand, knowing inherently that no one, other than I, could use it. I was the last of this fae family, not including Gruff, of course, but since he had been cursed to be a troll, he was no longer Grenfold, the would-be heir to the throne of McFeeny fae.

Damn my father!

Then I had this sinking feeling, like my heart had just dropped into my stomach. I couldn't really identify it, but suddenly my heart ached for my father. I didn't have time for him. There were two souls damaged by that cursed curse—Grenfold's and Coralie's.

Once again, I was thrown into this turmoil of wondering if

there was something I could have done. Maybe my failure to act was what really brought all this pain to my family.

Stop wallowing in self-pity, Teeny Weeny! You've got work to do.

I pulled out a silk scarf from my skirt pocket (all of my clothes have wonderfully deep pockets, thanks to Nina), carefully wrapped the heirloom in the scarf, and placed it back in my pocket.

The pixies were heavily engaged in dancing and rolling around in the shamrock, and I was grateful it kept them occupied. Gwynf'l, unlike most other lands in and around the Irish Sea, still remained charmed. The weather was quite mild for early April, the spring spirits obviously favored the land, and spring seemed to arrive much earlier than in most parts of this world.

I dug around in my carpet bag and pulled out my "crystal ball" to summon Seamus. He needed to connect with Coralie and let her know I was here. I would meet with her tomorrow at the point.

It was weird that I'd never thought to pair my ball with her pearl. Maybe I was afraid Father would then turn me into a troll, too. Maybe I was always *too* afraid.

I started, "Tahini McFeeny, Famous Seamus," praying to the spirits that he was receptive to my call. After several chants, the ball began to swirl into shades of green, and my dear uncle's face appeared through the rounded glass.

"Ah, Siobhan, my favored niece!"

Sheesh, I'm his only niece.

"Uncle Seamus! I'm here on Gwynf'l! Have you connected with Coralie?"

"Ah yes, lassie, that I have. She has been anticipating your arrival."

"Please let her know I will meet her at the point of the isle when the sun is directly above."

"I will do that, my dear! Stay safe! We all look forward to your return."

That was strange. What did he mean by "we all"? Only his son Mat was in Havenwood Falls. He must've meant it as a universal.

I whistled—well, it was sort of a whistle. It was a sound I could emit through my lips and teeth that only the pixie sisters could hear, kind of like a dog whistle, and generally they responded. Fortunately, as the sun was beginning to set over the mounts of the west side of the isle, they actually did respond, and the four little imps were by my feet in a matter of minutes.

I led the girls to the east side of the glen, where a thatched cottage sat, a bit dilapidated with a mountain goat perched on the roof, noshing on the few strands of decaying hay that still remained.

Ha! This is my family's castle. Our throne, our kingdom. So much different from Havenwood Falls, yet in so many ways, so much the same.

"Leave the goat alone!" I warned them. "We need to eat and get some rest. There is a lot to do tomorrow, and we have to head back home."

"Home, home sweet home!" Tierri started a chorus. Suddenly, the humble abode was filled with the shrill shrieks of four pixies competing in rounds, like a frickin' Christmas carol, "Home, home sweet home."

Dear gods and goddesses, spirits of the glen, give me patience and guidance.

Just in case, or just because I love faerie cakes, I'd also packed a few of them in my carpet bag (it was going to be a long flight, but since I slept through it, they went uneaten). I had also stashed some scones, compliments of Rebecca. This was the fare and sustenance of my people, and so we were well nourished for the night.

CHAPTER 6

*T*he morning greeted me with a bright ray of light from the eastern opening that posed as a window, sans glass. I blinked several times, trying to adjust my eyes to the new day's dawn.

Extremely loud snoring exuded from the far southwest corner of the cottage's single room, where the pixie sisters were all cuddled together, arms and limbs wrapped around one another in a faerie knot that no human could untie. I was glad my little sprites slumbered, unencumbered with the prospect of what might lie ahead.

I calculated that I had about four hours before the sun would peak above the point.

Stepping outdoors, I surveyed my surroundings. The glen was a few miles northwest of the point, and I could shimmer there easily, with few repercussions, but it wasn't worth taking the chance, *just in case*, since time was of the essence. Especially since the pixies didn't have any extra protection from the wards of Havenwood Falls, as they had stowed away unknowingly.

While the pixies slept, I donned the outfit I had on yesterday, since I was traveling light and didn't need to impress anyone. For that matter, I could glamour or affect anything or anyone I came across, but I had already become honed to the human nature of the world.

I checked out the carpet bag and remembered there were silk pouches of magic flakes that I must certainly have with me. This was the magic I knew. It may not have been strong, but it had served me well through the ages.

The time had come. My pixie wards had filled themselves on faerie cakes and goat's milk (don't ask).

I led them down the glen and to the shores of the Bay of Gwynf'l. We took a sharp left to the east, to avoid the village. The pixies, apparently satiated, followed me as if they were a small regiment following their leader. Here's the crux: I *was* their leader; at least that's what they thought. And they could think no different, spirits bless these little souls.

I saw the sun rising above the point. Tierri, Aeiri, Ushka, and Enya were on the shore, partly picking through shells and mostly wrestling in the sand, but totally engrossed in the semblance of a family picnic at the beach.

As I cautiously worked my feet over the rocky precipice leading to the promontory, I noted a storm brewing to the south. The edge of the southern sky was beginning to darken as if someone was taking a paintbrush filled with black ink and splaying it across the southern hemisphere.

I began the song. My voice was weak and tired. I was not very much of a singer, at least not anymore, but the words and the melody were the same, and Coralie was expecting me.

Of fish and reef and coral down under
Of shells and earls and Oceana's wonders

A fair maiden with hair a blaze of red
Lives here amongst this watery bed
With magnificent tail she swims the sea
I call to my dear friend Coralie

I watched as a great wave gathered, with aqua-colored sea-foam atop, moving fairly quickly toward the point. That would have been Coralie preceded by her glorious ancestor Neptune's regalia.

Out of the blue-green waters that lapped the point, a pale, almost pearlescent face, poked out of the ripples, followed by a cascade of rich orangish-red wavy tresses of hair that took hold of each wavering ripple and seemed to follow them.

Big bright green eyes like emeralds blinked at me, as the long reddish eyelashes batted back the bright sunrays that blazed upon the sea and rock. Her large pearl hung at the base of her neck, shimmering in the sunlight.

Neither of us knew who should speak first. Coralie had once been my closest friend, centuries ago. My brother Grenfold would never have known her, if she had not been my ally, my confidante, the sister I did not have.

Oh great! Another wave of guilt to deal with.

"Coralie, it's time to come home. You need to be with those who love you most. Are you ready?"

Unexpectedly, Coralie replied, "I've always been ready."

Relieved that she didn't protest, I pulled a small silk packet of faerie dust from my bag, along with my Tell All Ball. I waved my hand over the ball, and a hole developed, about three inches in diameter. I knelt over the rocky jetty and scooped up a batch of seawater into the ball. I had "divined" a fishbowl out of my crystal globe.

Before I could sprinkle any fae powder onto the dear forlorn mermaiden, the storm that came beckoning from the south approached briskly.

A small fishing boat in the distance tried vigorously to paddle ashore. A tall, lean, well-endowed woman with stark black hair stood at the bow, barking orders at the poor sailor trying earnestly to fathom the impending storm. Her stance and demeanor were familiar to me. Although she and the small boat were nearly a mile down the shoreline, my keen sight and smell detected that it was none other than Shayin Pisik, the vicious cat-shifter-witch who had been sent to her place of origin in the Carpathian mountains, after trying to slay my dear nephew Mat. Or so I thought, but here she was. A huge lump grew in my throat at the sight of her, nearly choking me.

No sooner had the vessel reached the beach than Shayin, with supernatural strength, grabbed the unwitting rower by the collar, lifted him off his feet, and ruthlessly slung him far into the cold deep waters of the bay. The taste of bile rose from my churning stomach, from either fear or the awful scent of the cat-woman, or both, making me retch.

The sight of her, the smell of her, so like my dreams, made me shake uncontrollably. My dreams—my omens—were true. Had I arrived only a little later, I would have been too late. In fact, my trembling caused me to believe I may still have been too late to save Coralie. I was certainly no match for the likes of the Pisik.

The witchy creature caught sight of us, too. I could see her visibly twinge—not exactly recognizing me, because of the memory wards of Havenwood Falls, but a twinge of something. Then I realized—it wasn't me she was reacting to, but Coralie.

My heart began to pound relentlessly, filling my eardrums with the roar of its fast-paced rhythm, outmatching the speed of my shaking hands and knees.

She broke into an Olympian sprint across the sandy shore, and as she did, her long legs shifted into those of a large wild cat, and she continued to shift up her svelte upper body. As her arms became the front powerful legs of a feline, she moved to all fours, and her head became that of a black panther. Her speed increased astronomically with her new form, and she was nearing the point where I stood near Coralie rapidly.

So determined to "kill the fish," she obviously did not realize she was crossing the paths of the pixie sisters building little sandcastles on the beach, completely unaware of the invader. My stomach took another turn at seeing my dear wee ones in danger of being trampled by this fierce beast.

I swallowed back the acrid taste and gave out a sharp whistle. The pixies raised their tiny heads in time to see the large cat approaching only feet before them.

Immediately, the four sand covered imps jumped onto the furry back of the creature and sank their sharp little teeth into her back and shoulders. Enya threw sand into her eyes, and Aeiri hung on to the Pisik's tail for dear life—with her teeth. I was suddenly filled with so much pride, seeing these small creatures with such enormous bravery.

However, it did not take long for Shayin to regain her composure as she reached back and grabbed Aeiri off her tail with her fangs, and with a swift turn of her head, she tossed the pixie into the rolling waves. My little white-haired wonder bobbed helplessly, as Pisik's muscular tail swatted Tierri and Ushka off her back and stomped them into the beach with her large paws. Now these two were clawing fearfully to get out of the sandpit that Pisik had just fashioned for them.

She then batted Enya on the top of her head, sending the hotheaded pixie into the rocks that lined the shore. Enya appeared dazed at first, then began to get her footing back as she lifted herself from the rocks. But the she-cat swerved back to go after Enya, and I could see the fire in Pisik's eyes far outburned whatever little Enya could muster, as she sped toward her to put an end to my poor little ward.

That was enough.

I grabbed my father's wand out of my pocket and pointed it at the vile vixen.

"To Hell with you, Shayin Pisik!" I screamed at the top of my lungs as a bolt of lightning flew from the tip of the brightly glowing wand. The recoil from the wand was so strong that it knocked me off the point, and I was flailing backwards into the icy depths of the sea.

As I was falling, only one thought filled my mind:

I've failed! I've failed! I can't save anyone, not even myself.

I closed my eyes to accept my fate, as my poor brother did centuries ago. But other than a spray of sea mist, I never felt the frigid grip of the waters. Instead, warm soft hands were holding me above the waves. I turned to look deep into Coralie's dark green eyes, and her beautifully soft smile shone upon me as she gently placed me back upon the rocky crag.

While a dark plume of black smoke rose high into the sky, dissipating into the jet stream above, I saw Tierra and Ushka brushing sand off of one another, and Aeiri twirling around as droplets of seawater flew from her pale pink skin. Enya was rubbing a blood-soaked spot on her head, but a huge smile on her face denied any pain. Then the four pixies broke into cheering and began dancing around in a circle.

I could almost hear the pixies singing "Ding-Dong! The Witch Is Dead" from *The Wizard of Oz*, but of course, that was my imagination. They were singing some faerie song of glorious joy.

I whistled once more to summon them to my side, and the four wandering minstrels came skipping toward me.

"You all were wonderful! So brave! I could not have done this without you!"

The pixie sisters beamed with pride and began patting each other on the back. Then the happy patting became a rabbit punch to one another's arms, and before one could count to three or four, they were all wrestling in the sand once again.

"Brother! Well, it's time to go," I said, so totally relieved that everyone was safe (if not exactly sound) as I tossed a sprinkling of faerie dust on the pixies just as a gentle wave lapped up to the shore, and the four wee women turned into four miniature minnows. I scooped them from the foamy remains of the retreating wave into my makeshift aquarium. I pulled a second packet of dust from my pocket and sprinkled that upon the waiting Coralie. She transformed into an iridescence of orange and white, with translucently flowing orange fins and tail, much like her hair appeared as a mermaid, becoming an elegant oriental Koi. She leapt out of the water and landed expertly in the Tell All Ball.

I waved my hand over the ball once more, and the opening that had appeared to allow the water in now disappeared, the ball becoming a globe once again.

I plopped the ball and the wand into my carpet bag and headed back toward the glen and the thatched cottage, once my family home.

I lay down on a small cot that I covered with one of my oversized scarfs. Setting the carpet bag beside me, I took stock of the now five wards I was charged with.

Good night, my little sea urchins.

I fell into a deep sleep, so exhausted from it all, and so relieved my swimming serpents were all safe.

CHAPTER 7

J had no idea how long I slept, but I awoke with a sense of overwhelming urgency. The Isle of Gwynf'l is filled with mystery and magic, and time on the isle is among those wonders. Years could flash by in a heartbeat, and days could last forever. So much time had passed since last I was here, I had forgotten its many mysteries.

I could not waste any time getting home. I decided I would shimmer to Boston. At least I would be back in the States without dealing with customs, TSA, and Homeland Security, especially with a freaky ball of fish in my luggage, and a flashing wand that would not stop glowing.

It was risky. That was a far distance to shimmer, especially with the load I was carrying, but I had to take a chance and hope that the Stipple in the Ripple would work to my benefit. After all, I was heading west, and the time zone would be five hours earlier. Maybe this time I would get lucky and so would the days be earlier in this ripple.

In Boston, my shimmering landed me in front of a People's Bank near the pier. A digital sign at the top of the bank scrolled bright red letters reading, "TIME TO SAVE! IT'S MAY 13, 2019, 8:27 P.M."

Oh jeez and jezebel, I've lost an entire month with all this shimmering! How long was that magic supposed to last?

The stars above the bay sparkled in the velvety night sky as their reflection glittered upon the waters. The smell of fish and salty spray filled my nostrils as I took in the surroundings. I passed my hand over the water-filled ball, and the opening reappeared. I went to the end of the pier and sprinkled a little faerie dust on the graceful white and orange koi that was swimming in the ball of water. The koi leapt out of the ball, and as it splashed into Boston Harbor, she became the lovely sea maiden Coralie.

"Take a few minutes, Coralie, and stretch your tail. But we'll have to be leaving very soon."

A few more sprinkles on the guppies, and the pixies once again became their jabbing and jabbering selves.

"Where are we?" they all chimed in unison.

"We're in Boston. Back in the United States," I informed them.

"What's a Boston?" asked Aeiri.

"It's a cream pie!" answered Tierri.

As was their little pixie style, they all started jumping up and down, and ran around hollering, "Pie! Pie! My oh my!"

Now I had four tiny pixies rolling and wrestling down the pier. Before they could make enough ruckus to attract attention, I threw a handful of faerie dust at them, and the wrestling turned into a flapping of tiny fins and tails on the wooden deck of the pier. I scooped the four small fish into my hand and plopped them back into the crystal globe.

I sang out a few bars of Coralie's favorite song into the night, certainly not as beautiful as Coralie can sing, but sufficient for her to hear the call. The stunning mermaid, her scales looking diamond-studded as they glimmered in the moonlight and the reflecting stars, appeared in the ripples right below where I stood.

"Thank you, Siobhan! I needed that swim. Now let's go home."

Home? Where was that again? Ugh! I hope I'm heading in the right direction.

A dash of dust sprayed upon Coralie's lithe figure, and the mermaid jumped out of the harbor and transformed into the small oriental carp once again in mid-air, splashing into the globe in a perfect dive.

All my wards safe and sound in the Tell All Ball once again, I shimmered to Logan Airport.

Wards? There's something about that word. It nagged at my memory, but I couldn't seem to put my finger on it.

I had a ticket stub in my carpet bag that showed Denver as the place I had left from, so that must be where I had to go to get back to Heavenbark Springs. *No, that's not it. Haven Tree Waters?* I wasn't sure what my town's name was anymore! How could I not know that? Could the ripple have scattered my memory chip?

I had to get back to the beginning. That was all I knew, and the plane ticket was the closest I had to know where that was. So I went to the same airline that was stamped on that stub to book a flight.

The next one wasn't until morning, but it wasn't too costly—a couple of hundred dollars, and I still had a little over $450 in my pocket. It would give me a chance to rest and arrive early enough in Denver to figure out where I was supposed to go.

The flight home was very turbulent. My stomach was so queasy, and my head was swimming in a storm of confusion. Speaking of swimming, I checked on my ball-turned-fishbowl to see how my little friends were doing. They appeared unaffected by the rock and roll of the plane's maneuvering through the turbulent skies, probably because their watery surroundings just flowed with the movements of the airplane.

A flight attendant caught me handling the aquatic crew, and questioned me about the ball.

"Oh look, it's like a snow globe. The fish are actually made of silicone, but they look so real, don't you think? I just had to have it." Hoping my response would be enough to satisfy the attendant's curiosity, I grinned up at her.

She nodded in agreement, and went to check on a passenger a few aisles back—I could hear retching and the rustling of a barf bag being manipulated.

My sentiments exactly, fellow traveler.

At last we landed, but my head did not stop swimming, and I wasn't even sure where we were. As I walked down the gangplank with my carpet bag held tightly to my chest, a large sign appeared that read *Welcome to Denver International Airport.*

Okay, good, I was in Denver, and on land, thank the gods and goddesses. But I wasn't completely sure why I was in Denver or really where Denver even was in connection with my home. I was still confused, but relied on that used plane ticket I found in my bag. The mountains I'd seen in the morning sun as we landed somehow felt right to me, too.

A brightly lit poster hung on the wall ahead, displaying a quaint town surrounded by mountains decked with ski runs. It looked almost familiar, but not quite. The sign advertised *Ski Aspen.* I wasn't sure where I was supposed to go—I still couldn't remember the name of my town—but this picture on the poster seemed to come so close to what I could recall that I thought maybe it was near my home.

I went to the restroom and ducked into one of the back stalls.

There I pulled out the Tell All Ball turned fishbowl, and sprinkled some faerie dust onto the four circling minnows. One at a time, each minnow jumped out of the bowl and landed on the bathroom floor as a pixie. A little more dust on each of their heads, and they glamoured into four small, seemingly innocent children.

"Okay, we've got to get moving. Any of you have an idea of where we need to go?" I asked, hoping maybe one of them would remember our hometown. I didn't even know why I thought any of them would remember, especially since they left home as stowaways, so they didn't get even get a smattering of ward magic to protect them.

Ah, that was it—ward, ward magic. That has something to do with why I can't remember home. I think.

While I was bending down to put the ball that still held koi Coralie back into my carpet bag, the four pixies crawled out under the stall door and took off.

Criminy, I need to run after these little imps like I need the hole I already have in my head.

As I exited the ladies' room, I caught sight of the men's room door closing, and what looked like a small pixie foot scooting inside. I looked around to see if the coast was clear, then ducked into the men's room to find Aeiri under the hand-dryer letting the warm air blow her cumulus locks around her face. Ushka was flushing the urinal and splashing around in the water.

"Look, Siobhan! I've never seen a fountain like this one before. Isn't it cool?"

"That's not a fountain! That's disgusting!" I pulled her out and placed her under the sink to soap her up.

Right at this moment, an older gentleman walked into the bathroom to find me and my tiny wards washing up.

"Sorry, sir. The girls can't read. We'll be out of here in a jiffy."

I pushed Ushka under the hand-dryer. Once dry, I grabbed

both Aeiri's and Ushka's wrists and dragged them both out of the restroom.

"You two stay with me. We have to find Enya and Tierri."

Ushka pointed across the large corridor filled with rushing travelers heading to or from their gates. I spied Tierri at a café concession, licking the apples and oranges in the refrigerated bin.

Oh, for Heaven's sake and Hell's fury!

I grabbed Tierri's hand and yanked her away from the fruit selections, and gave the cashier, who looked aghast, a ten-dollar bill to cover the Tierri-tainted treats.

"Where's Enya?"

Tierri, still licking her lips, pointed down the corridor to a large glass room, where Enya had her face pressed up against the glass.

Naturally, she's at the smoker's lounge, mesmerized by the curls of smoke and the little flames that fired up briefly and dashed out in an instant from the loungers' lighters.

Finally having rounded up all the wandering sprites, with my carpet bag slung over my shoulder, I followed the sign that directed me to ground transportation.

"Where to, lady?" the driver of the taxi we were ushered to asked.

"Umm, Aspen?" I responded.

"Wow, lady, that's a three-hour drive. Pretty steep fare for a cab ride. You don't want to take a bus?"

I looked down at my wayward wards and knew a bus ride with the four of them was out of the question.

"How much?" I gulped out the question.

"It'll be about half a K."

"Half a K? How much is that?"

"Five hundred, but the kids can ride for free, okay?"

Kids? Ha, if he only knew they were the ones he should be charging extra for.

"Yikes! Hold on." I fished around in my carpet bag to see what cash I still had left after the purchase of my plane ticket in Boston. I only had a couple of hundred dollars left, and that had to last me until I got back to the beginning. I felt around the bottom of the bag, and my fingers caught a plastic card lodged in the corner. I pulled it out and found what looked like a credit card, with the words *Havenwood Falls Savings & Loan* emblazoned on the shiny front of the card.

"Ah! Havenwood Falls, that's where I want to go! How far is that?"

"Sorry, ma'am. Never heard of it."

"Do you take debit cards?" If not, I could go back into the airport and find an ATM.

"Sure, not a problem. Still want to go to Aspen?"

"Absolutely!" I tossed the carpet bag into the backseat and guided the pixie sisters in along with it. I had a vague memory of a mountainous ride to Denver when I had left. The ride was eastward as the sun had begun to set behind us, and that trip seemed to take at least four hours, so Aspen just might have been close enough.

I handed him the debit card, as this was a trip he needed to be sure was prepaid.

The rugged looking cab driver—he kind of had that *I'm an ol' cowhand* look about him—ran the card, got the approval, and we were on our way.

CHAPTER 8

*T*he pixies had settled in the backseat right away, wrapped themselves around each other, and fell fast asleep. Except for their horrendous snoring, the long ride to Aspen was relatively peaceful.

The driver asked me about this unknown town of Havenwood Falls. Little clips of memories flashed in my mind, kind of like a movie reel with most of the frames skipping or missing. I couldn't tell him much really. It was a little like the picture I saw of Aspen, about the same size. The buildings were similar. I recalled gingerbread latticed Victorian homes, a town square with a large gazebo and a sparkling fountain, and thickly forested mountains surrounding the town. I started to tell him the people were very different, but my tongue got tied up before I could, and I wasn't even sure what exactly that meant.

Like me and the pixies, maybe?

He stopped in the center of town, next to an antique store. A good place to start, where I could ask people how to get to Havenwood Falls. I nudged the pixies awake, and they rubbed the sleepy sand out of their eyes. They tumbled out of the cab as I thanked the driver for the pleasant ride. He informed me he was going to check out some of the hotels and see if he couldn't pick up a fare back to Denver. I gave him a couple of twenties for a tip and wished him luck. The bills, having been nestled among some of my faerie dust, were likely to get him that fare in short course.

It was a bit of a risk, but I asked the pixies to split up in pairs and go into the shops to ask about Havenwood Falls. We were to meet right back here at the antique store in an hour. I pointed to a large vintage street clock at the corner of the sidewalk, and they eagerly nodded and headed in opposite directions, Tierri with Ushka, and Enya with Aeiri.

Earth with water, fire with air. May the spirits guide the sprites.

I started my inquiries in the antique store. There was a familiarity about the shop packed with old pieces of furniture, paintings, a rack of old-fashioned clothing, and bric-a-brac of all sorts and sizes. As I finagled my way through the boisterously positioned articles, trying not to knock anything over with my carpet bag, I came across a large painting of a rock jutting out of a tranquil body of water. The gold filigreed frame accented the sunlit sky reflected in the waters. Another ping in my memory banks— *Callie's? A picture of Coralie?*

An elderly shop attendant walked up to me and asked if she could help.

"Uh. Oh, sorry, by any chance do you know of Havenwood Falls? I think it may be somewhere near here."

"Havenwood Falls? Sounds intriguing, but I've never heard of it, and I've lived in these parts all my life. Hence the antiques." She giggled at her own joke. "I go out every weekend, generally a hundred miles or so in every direction, looking for that special treasure, but I don't recall ever being in a Havenwood Falls. Maybe I have, but I certainly have no recollection of it."

My disappointment was apparent to the kindly shop owner, so she suggested that I try the tourism bureau. Maybe I could locate the town on one of their various maps. She walked me out of the shop and pointed out the direction to the tourism bureau across the street and down two blocks.

I eyed the clock on the corner. I had another thirty minutes before meeting back with the pixies, gods willing. I headed toward the tourism bureau.

I passed by a pastry shop filled with delicious-smelling baked goods, by the scent emitting from its front door. My stomach rumbled, and I realized the pixies would be starving too, so I popped in to buy a few croissants and some sweet teacakes for the girls.

The dark-haired clerk at the counter had an interesting dragon tattoo that ran down her neck. A nose ring dangled from her left nostril in unison with another ring positioned on the end of her right eyebrow.

Maybe that's the kind of different I might've been telling the cab driver about?

After the clerk brought back a white paper bag filled with warm croissants and fondant covered treats, I took a chance and asked her if she knew of Havenwood Falls.

"Me and my guy take runs out on our bikes quite often. We love traveling through the mountains on the motorcycle, but really, I can't remember a place called Havenwood Falls. Maybe we did, but you know, so many little towns, they all kind of run into one another. Sorry, I can't remember it if we did."

Well, I tried. I paid for the pastries and headed out toward the Chamber of Commerce, where the tourism bureau was housed.

As I entered the three-story brick building angled on the corner, I spied a large map of Colorado hanging on the entryway wall. I went straight to the map and focused on the *YOU ARE HERE* marker. I ran my index finger along all the roadways through the area, looking for a star, a circle, or at least a dot, that signified a place called Havenwood Falls. There wasn't one.

A dark-skinned older man, a worker in a uniform with an embroidered *Aspen Chamber of Commerce* patch on the left side of his shirtfront, approached me and offered his assistance. The badge on his chest read *Brad*.

"Havenwood Falls? Sounds familiar, I think. There may be a bus that could take you there. Check it out at the bus station."

My eyes lit up, and I spun around with glee. When I completed my full circle, he was gone. I looked around at the other visitors, but Brad was nowhere in sight. I went to the visitor's desk and asked if they could find Brad for me, but the lady there said no one by that name worked here.

This was getting frustrating, to say the least.

A wall clock above the visitors desk warned me it was time to get back to the meeting place, assuming of course the pixies were paying attention to the time rather than fighting or playing amongst themselves.

Wonders of all wonders, I found four little tots punching each other on the arms when I arrived back at the antique shop. They stopped immediately upon the sight of me, and ran to me, grabbing my legs and hugging them so tight, I nearly lost feeling in my lower limbs.

"Okay, okay! We're all here! Anyone find out anything?"

Four mop-heads shook their tiny heads *no* in unison. Well, at least I had ghostly Brad's suggestion to go on.

So the five of us—well six, counting Coralie still housed in the fish-globe, smuggled away in my *rug*-ged bag—made our way down the aspen-lined street, heading for the bus station.

As we turned the corner, we came across an old-fashioned firehouse. A Sparky look-alike Dalmatian lay at the front door, licking his private parts.

How nice!

A small white sign with red edging and red lettering read *In an Emergency, Dial 9-1-1.*

Oh my gods and goddesses, why didn't I think of that? This is an emergency!

Once more, I fished into my carpet bag, no pun intended, and felt for my cell phone.

Although I really wasn't sure who would be on the other end when I called, there was something about 9-1-1 that rang a loud bell in my head, which probably sounded like the big red bell that was positioned over the red-lettered sign.

I looked at the phone, and three bars showed in the upper left corner.

Great! I have a signal!

I immediately dialed 9-1-1.

A worried woman's voice picked up and said, "Oh my gosh, Teeny Weeny! Are you okay? I've been worried sick about you!"

Teeny Weeny? This was no emergency operator, no "What's Your Emergency?" question. In fact, it was a much more informal answer, and the person on the other end seemed to already know what my emergency was.

"Who is this?"

"It's Barbie, Barbara Stuart, your best friend! Siobhan, are you okay? I think the memory spell kicked in, and the extension magic may have worn off!"

Well, she did say Siobhan this time. So I'm guessing she knows me.

"Where are you, Siobhan? We need to get you back to Havenwood Falls ASAP!" the voice on the other end added insistently. "You have family here! I mean more family, and then there's—" and she cut off.

Now she said that town name, Havenwood Falls. I must have known this Barbie woman. I was feeling like maybe I could trust her. Right now, there weren't many people I thought I could.

"Okay, assuming I know you, assuming you are my best friend . . . I'm in someplace called Aspen. But no one seems to know where or what Havenwood Falls is or how to get there."

"Well, of course not! You are so way out of the twenty-five mile ward radius around Havenwood Falls. You stay put! I'm going to send your nephew Mat to get you. You can all fly home as soon as he finds you."

"Havenwood Falls—no one seems to know where or what it is —but you are telling me this town has an airport?"

She did mention my nephew Mat, who was really my cousin, son of my aunt and uncle in Canada. It sounded like she knew something about him—that he was an owl shifter.

"No, silly, I mean Mat's owl will come and get you, and you can faerie-fly yourself home."

She knows Mat! She knows me!

I agreed to the plan, and she directed me on how to get to the Aspen National Park entrance. Mat would pick us up there.

It was nearing dusk as the pixie sisters and I arrived at the entrance to the park. I found a park bench to sit down on and let the pixies go climb the tall pine trees. This was the kind of environment that suited them well.

The sky darkened, and a sliver of moon shone in the night sky like a Cheshire cat's grin. Across the inky black sky, I saw a white bird coming nearer and nearer, with the pale moonlight bouncing off its outstretched wings.

Mat! Mathew! Mateus! Mathieu! (That last one is always pronounced like a sneeze, like Ma-choo!)

The handsome snowy white owl alit beside me. His amber eyes, like glowing Japanese lanterns, acknowledged me with such a sense of affection, it overwhelmed me.

I wrapped my teeny weeny arms around my rescuer, then noticed coming right behind him, out of the dark night sky, a glowing, iridescent green moth, the moonlight fully accentuating her glorious wings.

Mat turned his owl head in that eerie, nearly full-circle manner to eye the beautiful creature that trailed behind him, and nodded as he stretched out his wings and began to morph into the tall, bronzed beautiful human of himself.

He's amazing!

"Aunt Siobhan!" Now his large muscular arms wrapped around my whole body and lifted me well off the ground. Hearing his voice, the pixie sisters scrambled down their climbing posts. "And the pixies, too?" He shook his head, his white locks swinging as he chuckled. "Why am I not surprised?" He gestured at the beautiful moth. "I brought Cyllene along with me. She is one of your oldest friends. She always knows the way home. After all, that is where she was born, long before any of us ever came to Havenwood Falls. I'll take the pixies back to Havenwood Falls on my back, and carry your luggage for you. Effervesce, and Cyllene will guide you home."

Mat laid out the instructions for getting back to the *beginning* —back to *home*!

After Mat transformed himself back, in his glorious manner of turning from hair and muscle into feather and wing, I disenglamoured the four tots into their wee selves, and they all crawled through the down of the wings of this magnificent bird and onto his back, eager for the flight of their lives.

I'm pretty sure it is the flight of their lives!

Mat took flight into the moonlit sky with his four tiny passengers, grabbing the handles of my trusty carpet bag in his strong claws as he lifted off the ground.

Cyllene, who Mat had explained was a minuscule dryad, the soul of a tree, was buzzing and humming in a nagging way, urging me to effervesce. Although I could not really understand her, I knew instinctively that if I effervesced, I could become my flying fae-sized self.

I nodded and then my long brown hair began to turn solid white, starting from the ends and moving toward the roots. Once my hair became totally white, my skin paled, and the forest lit up with a light so bright that prismatic colors from all that whiteness bounced off the dark green needles, throwing the light into this small glade, making it like a ballroom with one of those mirror-type chandeliers. Thousands of small, effervescent bubbles began to rise from my neck, arms, and legs, and then I heard the familiar fizzle and a pop.

I now stood next to the mothy nymph who was perched on the park bench. I was just a head taller than her—my now teeny weeny head—but I was ecstatic to be able to look her in those stunning multicolored eyes of hers. I gave her a kiss on her colorfully pallored cheek. I couldn't help it; I felt so happy to be with someone who truly felt like a dear friend.

"Ready to go home, Siobhan?"

"Oh yes, Silly Annie!" *That* Silly Annie *just popped out of my mouth from nowhere.*

"I mean Cyllene," I added, making sure I pronounced it properly. *The Rain in Spain . . .*

She smiled, assuming I corrected myself purely for her benefit.

CHAPTER 9

*I*t felt as if we were sailing as Cyllene and I floated through the deep dark velvet night. She did indeed know exactly where she was going, and though I could fly much faster than her, I trailed back, allowing her to be my pilot and navigator. After all, I was the one who was lost.

Her bright luminescent wings were sails against a calm, unfathomable blue sea of night. I could never be so happy to follow those beautiful flowing tails of her wings, glowing in the incandescent moonlight.

The two of us flew through the protective ward of Havenwood Falls. Cyllene was unaffected, as she had predated by eons the founders who created the wards in the first place. I, however, felt an *almost* imperceptible squishy feeling, as if I had pierced a bubble, which was accompanied by a nearly inaudible *pop*. It was a sensation that I could only describe as a combination of my shimmer and my effervescing, if they could be combined. As soon as we passed through, my memories of my home returned fully, as though they'd never been gone.

Weird!

I would have expected Cyllene to lead me back to my townhome and shop on Main Street, but she did not. A little turn to the left past City Hall, and we arrived in front of a large Victorian style mansion. I recognized it immediately as the mayor's home. My mayor, my Barbie Stuart, my best friend (not counting Cyllene—or Coralie, for that matter).

How many "bests" can one have? Regardless, I must be home, because now everything is familiar.

As I alit on the bottom step of those leading up to the front porch of the mayor's mansion, Cyllene perched on the post of the railing. I effervesced with that same pop and fizzle, only now those clear bubbles were filling up with colors and growing much larger, as I morphed into my Madame Tahini, Teeny Weeny, Havenwood Falls demeanor. The voice I had heard on my cell phone in Aspen preceded the tall, large-haired Wonder Woman–looking person who stepped out onto the front porch.

She stooped down and immediately hugged me and lifted me off the stoop with ease, raising me way above her head, as if I were nothing more than a carnival toy.

Okay, granted I'm of small stature but REALLY? Barbie still hasn't told me everything, dragon pendant or not!

It was so good to be home. Now I felt like Dorothy in *The Wizard of Oz*. Yet there was still so much unfinished business. I still had a poor mermaid that was trapped in the body of somebody's pet fish. I still had my poor brother, trapped in the body of a troll. I still had this uneasy feeling that my father's power sat in my bag, uncomfortably vibrating emissions that I couldn't even grasp.

I now needed to just go to my home, my shop, my little townhome, my bed, my most comforting surroundings.

I begged Barbie's forgiveness for needing to leave so quickly. She never said a word, just set me down and turned me toward the direction of my shop on Main.

Now that is the definition of a true friend. They know what you need when you need it.

I opened the heavy wooden door to my townhome, feeling so exhausted that even pulling it closed seemed to be a great exercise. I heard familiar snoring resounding from the living parlor and found the pixie sisters all nestled in the overstuffed chair in front of the hearth. Mat was fast asleep on the settee, with his long legs dangling over the arm of the sofa. Even Cyllene had found a spot on the back of the settee to rest her weary head.

I went upstairs to my bedroom, where Mat had already placed my carpet bag. I would have to unpack, but not tonight.

Donning my comfortable flannel nightgown, I fell back on the down-filled mattress and was out.

I arose the next morning to find Mat in the kitchen, already brewing a cup of tea for me. He had sent the pixies back home to their forest haven with the faerie cakes from the freezer and sent Cyllene back to Maximus, her soul tree. The young owl shifter wisely knew I could use a little peace and quiet.

The two of us sat down at the kitchen table. I gave Mat a recap of the beach brawl with Pisik, and what I hoped was her final destiny. His amber eyes opened wide with amazement as I re-visualized the scenario for him.

"By the way, Aunt Siobhan, my father and mother will be arriving in Havenwood Falls in the next few days. They are on their way!"

"They are? That's terrific! I miss Seamus and Abigail so much! Seems my little family here in Havenwood Falls is getting bigger and bigger."

After we finished tea and Mat took off to start his day shift at Broastful Brew, I padded around the house for a bit, really doing nothing at all, until I could motivate myself to go back upstairs and unpack.

I placed the carpet bag on the bed and began removing items one by one, examining each.

The Tell All Ball was first, of course, and the brocade tablecloth. I set Coralie's temporary housing on the bedside table, under the Tiffany lamp. Next, I removed the sleek wooden box with the keyless lock, and set that down on the bed next to the bag.

A scarf here, scraps of paper there. The plane ticket stubs to and from Denver.

My cell phone, a few loose faerie dust packets, and my very handy Havenwood Falls Savings & Loan debit card.

A small light glimmered from the bottom of the case. My father's wand. I pulled it out and held it up in the dimly lit room. The tip on the end began to glow brighter, almost to the point that I could not even look at it, like looking into the sun.

The wand began to dim, my hand shaking nervously, as I held it reluctantly. *I'd better put this away.* I opened the box of magical stuff, moved aside the little packets of mysterious powders, and went to place the wand in the bottom of the box. That's when it hit me.

The crevice in the bottom of the box! That's for the wand! I could've realized years ago, when my father gave me the empty box for my faerie dusts, that he no longer had his wand.

"Coralie, I will have to take you to the Court later today so we can get you a tattoo to protect you. But right now, I think I need to see my friend Madame Luiza."

The small decorated carp flashed her translucent orange tail at me in acceptance.

I exited through the back door that led from the kitchen into my overgrown garden (I liked it that way). Even in winter, it seemed to flourish in abundance. I walked through the wooden gate attached to the old stones that father, Tess, and I had stacked meticulously.

I turned left down Beaumont Crossing—*Memory Lane, as Tess had dubbed it, from walking hand in hand with me and my father on our way to Danzan Park*—and headed to Whisper Falls Inn, a block away.

Whisper Falls Inn was a glorious three-story Victorian-style mansion, with a wraparound veranda, all the bells and whistles of the intricate lattice work for which that era was notable, and a large intriguing glass conservatory in the back filled with exotic flora, like a botanical garden. It occupied the entire block of Beaumont Crossing between Eleventh and Petran, as it included small cottages, similarly latticed, as independent suites for some of the guests.

Most folks referred to Luiza as Madame Luiza, and her nieces and nephew and their friends called her Mammie. For me, she was Luiza, the friend I had chatted with since coming to Havenwood Falls, over 120 years ago.

I did not have to ring the bell when I reached the front door. Michaela knew instinctively that I was on the porch (such is the Petran way), swung the door wide open, and held her arms out just as wide.

This beautiful child—well, not a child anymore—was as much my family as so many of the Old Families in this town. I knew their parents, their grandparents, and in some cases their great grandparents.

"Michaela, so good to see you, dear." I pronounced it *Mihaela*, like Luiza did. After all, I'd known Luiza, Mihail, and Irina long before this dear child was a twinkle or spark in their unique moroi eyes. "I think I need a visitation with Luiza," I informed her after our formalities were complete.

Michaela obliged graciously and escorted me to the familiar

parlor with the fireplace where Luiza and I had spent so many hours, years really, confiding in one another.

"A cup of tea, Madame Tahini?"

Before I could even finish saying, "Why yes, thank you," she had moved swiftly out of the parlor to brew a fresh pot.

I knew she thought Mammie's favorite place was in the room upstairs, but for Luiza and I, this was our "girls' night out" place, or as we called it, "Girls' Night Inn."

A cool breeze circled the room with a hint of lavender whispering upon it. A blurry vision began to appear, and then took full shape as the woman I knew for more than a century, dressed eternally in her favorite lavender-colored gown.

Madame Luiza.

"I see you found it." The apparition spoke—the deceased Whisper Falls Inn keeper, and Michaela Petran's aunt.

"Found what?"

"Your father's wand. His scepter."

"I did. It's strange. I never knew that he had left it behind."

"Your father was a very interesting man. He was stalwart, strict, and extremely stubborn. I suppose having to rule his fae may have accounted for some of that. But when your mother, Rose, died, a large part of him died with her. Your father was heartbroken."

"My father? He always seemed so ambivalent."

"Oh no, my dear! His guilt ran very deep. He felt great remorse for punishing your brother so harshly. Unfortunately, he could not find it in himself to reverse the curse. Maybe it was his stubbornness, or maybe he just didn't know how to undo what had been done. To add to that pain, his beloved Rose died of heartbreak over your brother's fate. Tess and I were very close friends. She confided a great deal to me."

"I never in a million years would have thought my father felt bad about cursing Grenfold."

"There's more, dear. That was his curse on your brother. The sins of the father are visited on the son and vice versa. Your father Ian, as hard as he tried to have another son, was cursed to lose all in childbirth. Each of his subsequent wives all lost their only child, a son, in childbirth. In fact, only Tess survived the birthing, though the baby boy did not."

"I don't think I was ever told that the babies were boys."

"Now you are the heir to his power. You have the wand to rule your fae."

"Rule my fae? There are not many of us left to rule over. Not sure even what that means."

"Things are ever changing, Siobhan. Already your nephew Mat has come to Havenwood Falls, and maybe more? And I know you have brought someone home with you."

"Ah, yes, that is true, but she is not fae. That was the whole trouble in the first place."

"Things are ever changing, Siobhan."

Now she sounds like a broken record.

"You have the power to break what was broken. Seek it within yourself."

Power! Bah! Everyone wants power, but it only seems to bring heartache.

A scent of lavender still trailed in the room after Madame Luiza's departure.

That sinking feeling I had at Grenfold/Gruff's rock came blasting back at me. With Luiza's recitation, all of a sudden, I realized what my father gave up. He traveled thousands of miles from our homeland, with his small clan in tow, but without the power he normally would've wielded if he'd had his wand with him.

I feel like such a dunce. A loser. So much time wasted, angry with my father, not ever caring that this man who tried to protect me and so many others, all these years, had so much love and grief in his heart.

All this time, I never thought of my father having feelings, of him loving anything but his power. Had I been that wrong about him? Was there really something I could have done to change things?

Ever changing?

∼

After I finished my tea at Whisper Falls Inn and thanked Michaela for her hospitality, I returned to my own home to prepare Coralie for her tattooing.

I opened my wooden box with a wave of my hand, the latch snapping open instantly, and took out a pink silk packet. Placing the makeshift aquarium on the bed next to the wooden casing, I poured a small bit of a pale pinkish powder into my hand and sprinkled that into the glass sphere.

The water in the bowl began to churn, and bubbles began to rise in rapid succession, filling the entire room with floating spheres of pink and purple that threw off the rays of light from the Tiffany lamp into a profusion of multicolored beams.

Within seconds, a beautiful woman appeared, with skin the color of fresh cream and bright red hair that flowed and waved like an anemone crowning her head. She was completely naked and was stretching out her new legs that had replaced her familiar tail.

"These are interesting," Coralie said as she wiggled her brand new toes.

I explained to the lovely sea maiden that I would need to take her to the Court of the Sun and the Moon to have Adelaide Beaumont give her a protective tattoo, one that would be infused with magic, the kind of magic only Addie would know was needed.

I took out one of my shawls from the armoire and wrapped it around this gorgeous creature, sarong-style. Although mid-May was still quite cool in our parts, Coralie was a cold-blooded animal, and it should suit her well. The shawl should be all she needed.

She followed me out of the bedroom and down the stairs, and I could hear her mutter oohs and ouches all the way down the steps.

"What's wrong, Coralie? Are you okay?" My healing instincts kicked in.

"I don't know. It feels like I am walking on nails and hot coals," she replied.

I hadn't thought about that. She was a fish, not a human. I recalled Hans Christian Andersen's story of the Little Mermaid and how she had to suffer the thorny pangs as she walked in her human body. I would have to get this over with as quickly as possible in order to transform Coralie back to her natural form and place her in a more comfortable habitat than the painfully rough surfaces she would experience on this earthly ground.

I led her straight across town square, keeping an eye on Coralie as she gingerly tiptoed through the park, around the fountain and to the other side. She winced at every step, and I could feel the prickles in my own feet. I felt so bad that she had to endure this.

Opening the heavy metal door to the Court, I led the aching woman toward Adelaide's office.

Introductions and background provided, Addie asked Coralie if she had any idea what kind of tattoo she might like.

"Maybe a heart with an anchor? That's how I have felt for so long, like my heart was dragged to the bottom of the sea."

There's that knot in my stomach again. So much heartache.

Addie said she didn't believe that would always be the case, and felt a design like that would only serve to keep it that way, a self-fulfilling prophecy, so to speak. She proposed a heart with wings and fins, and Coralie's eyes brightened, the pair of emeralds shining nearly as bright as they once did so many moons ago.

I told Addie that I intended to take Coralie to Peacock Lake at Small's Falls, especially since it was so close to my cabin, and I go there so frequently, especially in the spring and summer. The Court's manager reminded me the lake water there was toxic.

"Well, definitely to humans, and yes to some supernaturals, but I think since Coralie is a water-bound creature, she should be safe."

Addie said she would infuse the tattoo with magic that would protect her from the bear shifters and cat shifters, as they both were very fond of fish, and of course the humans would never be able to see her, even though most of the human folk didn't go near Peacock Lake, its legend being quite famous around town. But you never knew about the wayward tourist. And she would add a spell that would protect Coralie from any of the toxicity the waters may have for her.

"Just in case," she added with a wink.

I smiled at her comment. Addie, like a few others who had known me most of their lives, knew that "just in case" was my tag line. I was surprised they didn't call me Just In Case Teeny Weeny.

Coralie, with her new enchanted tattoo, stood up, and with a grimace, began to step toward the exit. Addie sensed her pain immediately, and with a flick of her fingers, tossed a spell at Coralie's feet.

Thank goodness Addie is so good at what she does. I've cast so little magic for so long, I didn't even think of it.

"Thank you! This is wonderful! It feels like I have little bubbles around my feet!" Coralie exclaimed joyously.

"Well, now you are sarong-wrapped, bubble-wrapped, and ready to go. Let's get some lunch," I said as we walked out of the Court of the Sun and the Moon, and she shook those bright red locks vigorously in agreement.

Back in my kitchen, I found some leftover faerie cake dough in the freezer and thawed it out, adding a little cherry Jell-O mix to the batch. I made small round balls of the cherry flavored dough and let Coralie suck on those while I brewed a pot of tea.

As soon as we finished filling ourselves up on most of the delightful doughballs, I gathered up some packets of faerie dust and placed them in one of the ubiquitous pockets of my skirt. Again we headed out of my townhome, this time through the back garden.

I instructed Coralie to hold on to me, as I would shimmer us up to Peacock Lake, and hold on to me she did, as she lifted me into her arms and cradled me like an infant.

The wavering air surrounded the both of us as we flowed into a translucent wave, then vanished, to reappear again at the edge of the lake.

Peacock Lake was so named as it fanned out from the triplet of falls that fed into it, known as Small's Falls, and the waters were mesmerizing bands of teal, green, blue, and turquoise. It looked like a peacock's tail in its fabulous array of colors.

I explained to Coralie, "You won't be alone in the lake. There's a sweet young water nymph, Mallory Dorian, who has an affinity to the lake, I've noticed. I think you will like her. I have a good feeling about her. There are also a few other water nymphs who may or may not show up, but I am sure you, of all mermaids, can handle the likes of them."

Coralie shed her sarong and sat on the edge of the lake, dangling her feet into the cool waters of the lake. I pulled out a light blue packet of dust and sprinkled a pale aqua powder upon her head.

The delicate toes at the end of her feet began to web together. She crossed her ankles, and a parade of glimmering green scales started to crawl up her legs, enveloping them into the full tail of the alluring Coralie.

She pecked a kiss upon my cheek, and in an instant, splashed into the waters of the lake, flipping her tail with glee, as she bid me good night.

I heard a baleful moan coming from the direction of Gruff's cave.

Forgive me, my goddesses, gods, and Gruff.

That sickening feeling overwhelmed me once again as I shimmered back home.

Another long day, and I went to bed that night completely worn out. I pulled out a light flannel set of pink pajamas scattered with dragonflies, to help drift me into a peaceful slumber. Crawling into my welcoming bed, I curled up with my favorite down pillow and cried.

I wept for Coralie. I wept for Grenfold and Gruff. I wept for five mothers and would-be brothers. I wept for my father, the king of our fae. I cried and cried until at last my teeny weeny head could cry no more and fell asleep.

I awoke at dawn, my pillow completely tear-soaked, the dream I had during the night still mysteriously rumbling around in my head.

This is ODD!

I retrieved my trusty cell phone and dialed none other than 9-1-1. And my trusty friend on the other end answered before the second ring could even start.

"Siobhan! Don't tell me, another dream?" the mayor's inquisitive voice started the conversation.

I nodded, as if she could see me, and asked her to meet me at Broastful Brew, as usual. Nothing too urgent—we could meet at our regular time.

And so it was, Barbie and I sitting at our familiar table a little past eight, with Mabel chatting away, and Mat behind the counter, preparing our beverages.

"So spill it! You have me stayed in suspense, Siobhan," Barbie said, accentuating every *s.*

That's my best friend, doing her best to alliterate for me.

"It's so odd, Barbie. I mean, I'm sure it's because of bringing Coralie back here and knowing how hard this is for Gruff."

I gave her the rundown on the adventures in Gwynf'l, finding my father's wand, the wicked witch of a Pisik and her near total destruction of us all, my crazy confused trip back home to Havenwood Falls, and even my chat with Luiza.

"Well, that was quite a trip. Even Bent Brent would be proud of you! But you still haven't told me about the dream last night. That is why you called, right?"

"Yes, actually. See if this sounds familiar. My father chanted the code, 'We, this family of fae, are of earth and air. When sea mixes with earth, it becomes mud. When sea mixes with air, tears fall from the heavens. You have brought both to this family. To be true, from this day hence, no longer are you fae, a prince. For your crime I extol, from this day forward, your life, a troll.'"

"That's your spring equinox dream. I hear of it every year, so yes, very familiar."

"Yeah, well I had it last night! Long past the spring equinox. In fact, we're coming up to the summer solstice shortly." Ha, I got my alliteration in there, too.

Oh no! I missed May Day and Spring Fest for the pixie sisters! I will have to make it up to them this coming solstice.

Barbie looked pensive, then she got her invisible detective's cap on and said, "Was it the whole dream or just that part?"

"Just that part, why?"

"Siobhan, I told you before, you have more power than you give yourself credit for. Even Luiza is trying to tell you that! You told me she said, 'You have the power to break what is broken.' The answer is in your father's curse. You have to seek it."

So many broken records around here. Break what was broken? Seek it?

I just nodded as I dipped my teabag in and out of the tiny teapot in front of me.

How come my friends can see what I can't? I mean, I'm not surprised by Luiza. After all, aside from her supernatural life, she is in the land of spirits now. But Barbie, my human (maybe) friend? How can even she see things that should be as clear as the nose on my face, as small as that might be?

We finished our little café klatch, and bid each other a good day.

I wandered down the blocks of town square heading back to my place, but the only thing that kept ringing in my head were the words: *break what was broken.*

Come on! How do you break something that's already broken? It really didn't make any sense, but apparently it did to some people and apparitions. Okay, maybe I needed to parse the words, so to speak.

Break! Break! Break! My father placed a curse on Grenfold. I had always wished I knew a way to break the curse.

Wait! Didn't Luiza say he may not have known how to undo what was done?

So the first word was break—I needed to break the curse. Okay, that was easy to figure out, kind of like the nose on my face. But if the curse hadn't already been broken, then what was broken?

Broken? Broken? Broken?

By the time I got home, my head was breaking. I went straight to my bedroom to lie down, even though it was only mid-morning. I looked around the room, realizing it was still totally in disarray. I had been so occupied with getting Coralie to Court, then to Peacock Lake, I hadn't straightened up the mess. I had just gone to sleep last night with everything still piled up on my bed.

I went to pick up the Magical Stuff Box, and the wand, now sitting comfortable in its customary place, began to glow brilliantly.

The wand cast these words into the air, and they hovered like a neon sign over the center of my bed.

We, this family of fae, are of earth and air.
When sea mixes with earth, it becomes mud.
When sea mixes with air, tears fall from the heavens.
You have brought both to this family.
To be true, from this day hence, no longer are you fae, a prince.
For your crime I extol, from this day forward, your life, a troll.

That's it! Broken! Hearts are broken. Grenfold's, Coralie's, even my mother Rose's! I know how to break the curse! Thank you, my souls and spirits!

I effervesced to Peacock Lake, my father's wand—*No! my wand—* in hand.

Once re-effervesced into my Teeny Weeny self, I threw a few of the cherry dough-balls that I had kept in reserve into the lake. That's really all it took to summon Coralie to the surface.

Fish! Really, they are so easy to please.

"Coralie, I am sure I can fix this! Break the curse, bring Grenfold back to you! But I need your help!"

She looked at me with those curious emerald eyes, a little glimmer shining. Maybe the rising sunlight from the east catching a reflecting ray—or maybe more?

81

"Whatever you need, Siobhan. Tell me."

"I need you to sing your love song. The one that Grenfold and you have cherished for an eternity."

That reflecting ray in those emerald eyes disappeared. Her shining smile that greeted me at first turned to a fretful frown.

"It's okay! You can do this! I can do this! I need you to sing!"

Coralie lifted the giant pearl that always hung from a golden chain around her neck and let the rays of sunshine catch its special glow. And then it began.

Coralie, like the being she was created to be, began softly, soulfully, sounding like a true torch singer sitting on the top of a grand piano in a smoky bar, feeling the notes at the bottom of her heart, but emitting from the bottom of her lungs.

"My true love. My Grenfold, forever.
It's you I want, now and forever.
To be of your world, or you of mine
Love's magic would make it shine.
Alas, my beloved but it seems to be
My heart always anchored at the bottom of the sea?
My poor dear lover, do you see?
Are we destined never to be?
Neptune knows I'll never love another.
Grenfold, my soul mate, my only other.
My other half
My rod, my staff"

The tune, so mournful yet so loving, wafted through the forest of Mount Alexa. As I suspected, dear Gruff, the poor misshapen being, could not resist their song of love, his heart's desire that Coralie sang.

Gruff emerged from his cave and stumbled through the dense forest and pine-needle-strewn path down to the water's edge on rickety legs and gnarled feet. But the painful expression on his face told the truth that it was not the grotesque arrangements of limbs and bones, but his heartache that tore that slash of a mouth on his face into an excruciating grimace.

Gruff's tears fell like tiny pebbles running from a river brook. They hit the edges of the lake as he stepped up to the ledge and pondered the woman in the pond. His recognition of the water-bound woman as his true love Coralie made him cover his face with his arthritic-looking hands. He did not want his lilting love to see him, though it appeared that he doubted she would recognize him like this.

I thought he was about to plunge himself into the poisonous waters of Peacock Lake, but Coralie's first look at Gruff, at Grenfold, said it all.

Her emerald eyes sparkled, then softened, and her luminous smile grew wider. One could almost feel her rapid heartbeat as unaccustomed waves began to form in what was always a very still body of water.

Coralie did not see Gruff. What she saw was her beloved Grenfold. She knew and felt his soul. This creature of true beauty did not see a mottled skin, warted, and malformed troll. She saw her own true love.

I knew this was the moment of truth. I pulled out my wand and placed its glowing tip upon Gruff's forehead and said:

"We, this family of fae, are of earth and air.

When sea mixes with earth, it becomes clay with which to build.

When sea mixes with air, it becomes rain with which to grow.

Let sea, earth, and air become the love that builds and grows.

The spring spirits bless us all."

I watched and listened to the transformation of poor Gruff becoming Grenfold once again. This time it was not the horrific crunching of bones, nor the sad transformation of a spirit's ethereal fae eyes turning into lumps of coal. It was a symphony of such astronomical proportion that it seemed as if all the angels of the universe were strumming their golden harps in unison and all the songbirds of the forest joining in joyful harmony.

The next moment, Gruff had become Grenfold once again, my beautiful, handsome fae brother. But something had changed. A softer look in his eyes, not like the arrogant bright hazel ones of yore. They were still hazel, but softer shades of gold and green folded into the browns of his irises. Perhaps his years as a troll had humbled him.

By my side stood four little pixies staring at the wand in my hand, and Cyllene on my shoulder, just nodding in a self-righteous sort of way.

Grenfold kissed me on my forehead and said, "Thank you! Make amends with Father! I love you always, sister!"

And with that, he dove into the lake, and the two lovers, who were always meant to be, swam into the depths of the precarious waters of Peacock Lake, now protected by their own hearts.

"Wait! Coralie, I have one more thing to fix!"

Coralie popped her head out of the water with an immensely joyous smile taking over her fair face.

"Your pearl. Hold it up."

Coralie did so, and with that, I tapped my wand on the lustrous orb and chanted,

"Spirits above and beyond, unite our call

The Whirling Pearl and the Tell All Ball"

By now, the four pixies were jumping, jiving, and oh yes, wrestling for glee over this way-too-romantic scenario.

"Well, now what are we supposed to do?" said the eternally grounded Tierri, after all the romping and raving.

"Well, Gruff, I mean Grenfold, is going to live with Coralie happily ever after in Peacock Lake, as they were meant to be."

"No, I mean what happens to HimaLaLa, the yeti that lives with Gruff? And what happens with his cave? Who's going to take care of HimaLaLa?"

"I wanna live with HimaLaLa!" piped up Aieri, interrupting Tierri's wave of questioning.

"Me too!" said Ushka. And so the numbering followed.

"Well, it only makes sense that you should all move in to Grenfold's—I mean Gruff's—cave, and care for HimaLaLa. After all, you are the ones who wanted HimaLaLa to stay here in Havenwood Falls."

Out of the clear blue sky, four tiny brooms seemed to have fallen into the pixies' hands, and the next thing I knew, they were headed off to the hole in the mountain, to sweep up and groom the gruffly honed ground into a home for the pixies and a poor unsuspecting yeti.

And that, Dear Diary, is just one of the reasons Havenwood Falls lives magically ever after!

Love and joy to all,

TW Tahini McFeeny

That's strange. I never sign my name so curly. Hmmm . . . Ever changing, Siobhan, Ever changing.

We hope you enjoyed this story in the Havenwood Falls series featuring a variety of supernatural creatures. The series is a collaborative effort by multiple authors. If you enjoyed meeting Addie Beaumont, read more about her starting with *Forget You Not* and *Lose You Not,* then continuing with her own story in *Break Me Not,* all by Kristie Cook, as well as *The Collector: Awakening* by Kristie Cook, R.K. Ryals, Belinda Boring & Nadirah Foxx.

Also look for the YA line, Havenwood Falls High; the historical paranormal line, Legends of Havenwood Falls; the sexier side of town, Havenwood Falls Sin & Silk; the local supernatural college, Sun & Moon Academy; and the Havenwood Falls holiday short story anthologies.

Stay up to date at www.HavenwoodFalls.com

ABOUT THE AUTHOR

T.V. Hahn has loved the fantastical and whimsical since she was a child, which may or may not have been that long ago. A creative soul, she enjoys making art with her hands, her voice, and her words. She finds humor in everything and is the first to laugh at her own jokes. During her downtime, you may find her tending her floral beauties, writing poetry, working on her faerie gardens, or watching *The Dark Crystal* or *The Princess Bride*. All of this, combined with her petite stature, has made more than one person wonder if she is, indeed, a faerie. It may be no accident that her first published book is about Teeny Weeny Tahini, a Spring Fae living in Havenwood Falls. Hahn is self-employed and lives in Florida with her husband and pup. She can be reached through her publisher, Ang'dora Productions.

ACKNOWLEDGMENTS

First and foremost, I want to acknowledge my publisher Kristie Cook, who believed I could really write in this genre, and led the way skillfully and gracefully. My editor Liz Ferry, who endures my incessant rhyming and alliteration and now has to deal with me writing in first person.

I'd like to thank Randi Cooley-Wilson for her allowing me to play a joke on Roman, suggesting how to do it, and cracking me up in the process. I also want to thank J.L. Weil for not only writing about Peacock Lake, but for discussing the story with me long before either of us had started our books.

Brynn Myers, an angel in her own right, who trustingly accepted my talisman. Tish Thawer for being *Witch and Famous*, and all the other wonderful authors in Havenwood Falls who collaborate and enrich my stories.

AN EXCERPT

Toil & Trouble (**A Havenwood Falls Novella**) **by Melissa Wright**

A cursed witch unable to use her powers. A shifter who's lived this long by keeping to himself. A choice to save her—or himself.

Circe is a witch. Everyone says so. Her powers have yet to manifest, but even if they did, an ancient curse prohibits her from using them. She's also an orphan, and the coven that raised her reminds her of both every day. Lest she fall in love and very bad things will follow.

Yearning for a break from the coven's rituals and meddling, Circe strikes out on her own in Havenwood Falls, far away from the constant reminders that someone wants her blood.

Evan is that someone. He's a shifter—a truth he's hidden his entire existence, and the single reason a council of mages hired him. And now, thanks to an unfortunate and binding deal, Evan has been charged with locating Circe. He should have dealt with her ages ago, but he keeps finding excuses not to. And it's not only that he doesn't trust the council's motives, or that he has no interest in kidnapping an innocent girl.

This job is all he needs to resolve his bargain, yet Evan can't seem to follow through.

When the council tires of waiting, they take matters into their own hands. And Evan must decide: step out of the shadows to save her, or keep his own skin.

TOIL & TROUBLE

BY MELISSA WRIGHT

He was supposed to take her. He hadn't. Five weeks and he hadn't. And now she'd gone into hiding, in a secret town nestled in the mountains of Colorado. Havenwood Falls: a haven for supernaturals. A place where she could have stayed safe indefinitely, if only he hadn't followed her.

He was a fool.

Circe was cursed. Alone. And that was the way she liked it. Love was for fools, not someone like her. She had better things to do, she thought as she shoved her dirty clothes into two machines at the back of the local laundromat. She'd spent most of her life not needing to remind herself of the ancient edicts holding her magic and love life for ransom, but after a few days in Havenwood Falls, suddenly she was surrounded by shifters and supes with Adonis bodies and secret, sexy-times smiles. It was getting hard to stay focused.

A shifter of some sort leaned against the machine beside her, his thick arms flexing as they crossed over his chest. She couldn't tell what kind, but he radiated otherness, and everything about him tried to draw her in. She reached up to amp the volume on her earbuds and slammed the door on the washing machine a little too hard. *Fools*, she reminded herself. *Love is for fools.*

And dirty sexy-time was how you got there.

Laundry Playlist blaring in her ears, Circe turned to go. She'd grab coffee while she waited on the wash; that would at least get her away from the half-dressed blond who liked to practice stretching his quads during the spin cycle.

The apartment she'd moved into at Havenwood Village wasn't quite ready when she'd arrived, but if she could only hang on a few more days, she would finally be able to close herself in and introvert the hell out of it. As it was, a nice man from McCabe & Sons was banging and hammering around four or five hours a day to whittle down the extensive list of damages left by the previous occupant. Whatever had happened there hadn't been an easy thing. Circe couldn't be sure if it'd been caused by one supe or two, but signs pointed to a violent and unintentional shift in the center of a crowded apartment—and it hadn't gone well. Being exposed to new species was turning out to be a good reminder to Circe to be grateful for what she had—at least her magic wouldn't tear her apart.

She strolled down the sidewalk toward Coffee Haven, tugging her new puffer jacket tight around herself. She wouldn't miss the soul-scorching heat of an Arizona summer, but this "cool mountain breeze," as her new hosts had called it, was a pretty harsh swing. Piles of snow edged the town where the streets and sidewalks had been cleared, and Circe imagined there would be long stretches of winter where she did not even leave her home. Havenwood Falls had something else that desert town didn't have: a hefty population of supernatural beings.

Thanks to a nasty curse, Circe's mother had died during

childbirth, leaving Circe orphaned. Well, that hadn't exactly been what had orphaned her. Circe had been told that once her mother was gone, her father couldn't stand to look at the child they'd created. He'd apparently abandoned Circe, left her on the steps of on old church inhabited by witches. Circe might have understood if he was too distraught to deal, but it was kind of hard to forgive something like that. Even now that the passage of time had given her distance from it.

Her father had dumped her, simple as that, and Circe had been left with nothing but a hand-me-down hex and a bad outlook.

So the witches who raised her became her guardians, and she counted the days until she was finally old enough to look out for herself. They'd insisted she call them all aunts, and she did love them, but some days they felt a lot more like jailers than kin. She'd played in the courtyard behind the church as a child, locked inside by invisible wards. The aunts had attempted a few play dates, but it was hard to find children who fit into a world so filled with magic, who would play among the church's crypts and lofts. So the cats and crows became her only friends.

She didn't know her birthday, but Circe had watched the calendar since she was big enough to read, and every March during the spring equinox ritual, she'd mark another year's passing. Eighteen of those ceremonies had come and gone without freedom.

And then, only weeks ago, a distant relative of one of the aunts had come for a visit. Lyra Beaumont had been pretty and petite, and pale enough it was clear she'd not lived through a recent Arizona summer. The aunts had met privately with her for long hours, and then they'd brought Circe in to be introduced. Circe had stood frozen in front of Lyra where she sat in a plush velvet chair, and it was gently explained that Circe would finally be allowed to leave their home.

Her heart was in her throat, but she still heard the truth of it. The offer came with a condition: she would be trading one set of wards for another. Circe could leave the coven, choose her own vocation, and live a real life, but only if she would come to Havenwood Falls, a place where she and her secrets could be protected. Lyra and the Beaumont family were apparently locals and members of the Luna Coven. Their coven and the governing body of the town—the Court of the Sun and the Moon—had been told of Circe's curse and her unusual situation.

The problem with not having a family is that you've got no one to ask what the hell you are. Circe's father had left her when she'd been no more than a baby. The aunts had found out what they could about him, and about Circe's curse, but it wasn't much. No one could be certain what might happen in her future.

Sure, the aunts had given her shelter until she reached an age where she could legally go out on her own—and even longer. They'd shown her what not to do. They'd shown her who to stay away from. They'd warned her of the curse, that she could never fall for a man or she would be doomed worse than her mother. But aside from that, aside from the constant assurances that she was a witch and that was all that mattered, they'd no idea where Circe really came from—what sort of beings her parents were. Circe knew she wasn't part shifter or vamp like some of the locals here. Not fae. But even though she hadn't come into her full power, something potent was inside of her. She felt it—the magic that ran through her blood, strong and dangerous.

Capable of decimating the shadows that followed her.

And, unlike the aunts, Lyra and her coven were not keeping Circe tucked away.

A chime dinged on the street in front of her, the door to Shelf Indulgence opening as a tall brunette came out. The woman smelled of herbs and tonics, and something like home. Circe didn't want to go back, but it was hard not to miss a place she'd been for nineteen years. Circe smiled, and the woman gave her a friendly wave, fumbling her books and packages before regaining control. One door down, and Circe was at Coffee Haven, near the center of a line of shops that faced the town square.

It was lovely inside, with worn hardwood floors and a long marble counter like an old-fashioned ice cream parlor. The walls were covered in art, hanging plants and crystals were scattered around the space, and Circe was comfortable despite the press of the crowd. She leaned against the counter, deciding on a sweet orange tea before being talked into a blueberry scone by a petite blonde whose name tag read "Willow." Circe had encountered the woman the previous day and noticed she seemed exceptionally good at reading people, that she had an uncanny intuition. There was a sense of otherness about this Willow, and Circe wondered if she had empathic abilities. Circe had been a bundle of nerves that first day, and Willow had immediately offered a selection of calming teas and sweet cakes.

Circe had liked her right away.

Today, Circe took her purchases to a small table against the wall and was immediately glad she chose the scone. Her gaze wandered over the crowd, taking in a myriad of supernatural tells and what appeared to be simply normal human beings, all going about their lives as if this wasn't an entirely epic event. Circe being alone. On her own. Thoroughly without the watching eyes of her many, many aunts.

Her gaze trailed over the wall of art, pencils and acrylics and oils, all varied in style and skill, and she realized they must have been the work of local artists. Her stomach dipped at the idea of the possibility, and she added it to the growing list of potential thrills: someday seeing her own watercolors on display. In public. She caught herself grinning like an idiot and bit the edge of her lip against that grin. Didn't want the residents of Havenwood Falls to think she was one of *those* witches.

And then a shadow moved at the edge of the storefront window outside, and Circe's mood fell. She wasn't under the watchful eye of the coven, but that didn't mean she was alone.

It didn't mean she was safe.

Circe grimaced, keeping her head down as she finished her scone. The tea was sweet, with just a little bite, and it warmed her all the way through. She thought she was brave enough now for her meeting with Addie, so she picked up her handbag overstuffed with elixirs and charms thanks to the vigilant aunts, and left the safety of Coffee Haven to tick off one more task.

Adelaide Beaumont, youngest of the Beaumont witches and Lyra's daughter, was not what Circe had expected. The aunts had called her a business manager and court liaison, but here she was in a hoodie and ripped jeans, legs crossed at the ankles with a worn pair of Chuck Taylor All Stars propped on the edge of the desk.

She snapped her gum, sitting up to give Circe a knowing smile as she spotted her in the doorway.

"Do I look that nervous?" Circe asked.

Addie chuckled. "It'll be over in a jiffy."

Circe managed to smile back as she looked at the woman, searching for signs of familiarity. Addie was a Beaumont too, which meant she was some distant relative of Morgan, one of the many "aunts." Morgan had never specified the exact relationship, but it was apparently close enough that the Beaumonts would do her this favor, that they would allow Circe a safe haven even knowing she would soon develop dangerous powers.

Circe cleared her throat. In truth, it wasn't the needle she was afraid of. "So this is permanent?"

Addie glanced up from the supplies she was laying out on the table, her wrists layered in bracelets and stones. She cocked a brow behind her black-framed glasses. "Already planning on running away?"

Circe took a deep breath and stepped forward. "No, I'm here for good."

She reached a hand out to Addie, cementing her independence from the aunts, committing her soul to Havenwood Falls.

Evan followed her as she walked alone through the town, apparently unaware of the danger she was in. Circe Alexander— nineteen years old, five foot four, brown hair, brown eyes, no identifiable markings—had been under the protection of thirteen women since the moment he'd found her, and now suddenly she was strolling around on her own, like she didn't have a care in the world. She'd been doing laundry, having coffee, browsing books, and now it looked as if she was sporting a brand new tattoo. So much for no identifiable markings. It was utterly baffling. And yet, here he was, watching her still.

Tattoo still fresh and pink, Circe sauntered along the town square, rubbing her hands and blowing a breath to warm them. It wasn't overly cold, but she was a transplant, and that made all the difference. Evan wore a jacket over his henley, but only so he could turn up the collar in an effort to blend in. The magic in his blood kept him warm enough, and the jacket had done little to keep him under the radar. This was a town scattered with supernaturals. They could sense their own. They knew he was something different.

Nothing about this bargain was going the right way, and every fiber of Evan's being told him to run. But Evan couldn't run. He'd made a deal. The thing about deals with mages is that they're unaccountably binding. Impossible to break. And, more often than not, started and ended in blood.

Evan ran a finger over the scar at the base of his thumb. He'd been desperate when he'd sought out the mages, desperate enough he hadn't thought about how dangerous they were—and foolish enough to think his life could get no worse. And then they had marked him, ran a ritual dagger across his palm before he realized what they'd done. They had his blood.

They wanted hers.

Circe turned into the laundromat and a cat shifter—probably Evan's least favorite kind—held the door for her, leaning too close and giving Circe a pointed smile. She ducked her head and pressed the earbuds into her ears. Evan waited as she folded her clothes and tucked them into an oversized tote, tugged the straps onto her shoulder, and headed back for the door. She had one more stop: the vet's office, where she would be picking up what might have been the ugliest bulldog Evan had ever seen.

When she finally stepped out of Havenwood Falls Animal Hospital, Circe knelt beside the beast, cooing and babbling and carrying on about how wonderful he looked. "He's got the prettiest trimmed nails and the softest coat, and he's such a good boy." And then she kissed him. Full on, right over his big slobbery mouth. The dog smiled, or appeared to, his maw going wide and his tongue lolling out as he panted. Chompers, it seemed, was also not too cold in the mountain climate.

Circe appeared to suddenly realize she was kneeling on a public sidewalk, her recently washed tote of clothes in danger of spilling and her purse abandoned in her haste to lavish praise upon this dog. She gathered her bags onto her shoulder and gave Chompers one final *good boy* pat. He waddled to standing, following obediently on his purple-patterned leash. They walked down Petran Street the few blocks to her apartment, and Evan found an alcove on an adjacent building, settling in to watch the door.

His cell phone buzzed in his pocket, but he did not check the screen. He knew what it was going to say.

There were no more excuses, no more chances to buy time. He

was going to have to do it. Tonight would be the night. The mages were on a deadline, and there was no way he could wait any longer and remain alive. It was her or him, and as much as it turned his stomach, Evan wasn't stupid. If he didn't hand her over, someone else would.

And they might not be as gentle about it.

He ran a palm over his face, thinking through his plan for the dozenth time. Second floor window, while she was asleep. Tainted rag over her mouth, band of herbs around her wrist. The mages had sent him with an arsenal of spelled weapons for one single woman. *She's dangerous*, Lucius had told him, the head of the powerful council taking the time to warn Evan himself. *Do not give her a chance.*

That was the thing that had stuck with Evan the most. The thing that had made him hesitate that first day. Dangerous, they'd said. A killer, no mercy, no code. Evan knew about witches. He'd had firsthand experience with the way they could destroy lives. He had been fully prepared to do what the council had asked, and then he'd seen her in the yard of the old church that housed the coven, and he'd wondered if that could ever be true. If Circe the witch could really be dangerous.

She had been reading in the morning sun, legs crossed over a blanket in the landscaped yard out back of the old church. One of their many cats sat beside her, preening until its black fur glistened like wet lacquer. Evan had watched as a small bird alighted on the stepping stones, not ten feet from that very cat. Circe's gaze had flicked to it, and the bird became hidden by a cloud of gray smoke until it lifted once more into the air. Spared from the keen eyes of the cat, just like that.

Dangerous. A killer. Eater of the hearts of men.

Savior of tiny birds.

Reader of historical fiction.

It wasn't as if Evan had trusted the mages to begin with, or even wanted to do their work, but when he made the bargain, he'd had no other choice. If he didn't do something, the magic inside of Evan would destroy him. He'd meant to gain freedom from a drawn-out, torturous destruction in exchange for completing a single task for them. Taking down a witch—a ruthless killer—seemed less an offense than stealing a harmless girl. So he'd waited. He'd watched her. That day, and the next. Nothing had ever changed in her, not even when under stress. Circe had never used magic again, aside from that first day, and Evan began to wonder if he'd seen it right at all. When she'd found herself in sticky situations with her guardians, when she'd been caught out in the rain, troubles large or small—never once did she reach for that power, never once did she use it to help herself or to hurt a soul.

Evan had made a bad bargain. He knew that much for sure. And now it was time to pay the piper.

Now, he was afraid, he was about to kidnap an innocent girl.

Purchase *Toil & Trouble where books are sold.*